AXEL'S

CHALLENGE

DAVE MARKS

NATIONAL WRITING INSTITUTE

ISBN 1-888344-34-2

For information on discounts for classroom sets or for institutional use, write National Writing Institute, 624 W University #248 Denton, TX 76201-1889

AXEL'S

CHALLENGE

DAVE MARKS

ACKNOWLEDGMENTS

I wish to acknowledge the help I've received from writers who have shown me how to maintain a value system, for this has taught me how to explain to young people how they can successfully keep and use their values, making them beneficial for themselves and others.

AUTHOR'S NOTE

I began writing this third book relating Axel's adventures with a telling of the events that completed his story. I was having some trouble getting started, but, fortunately, in an old trunk, I found a few pages of dusty and brittle paper that looked as if they might have been the start of a history of some sort. They were in Sidney's spidery script and hard to read, but using them saves me a bit of work so I've included them.

Those of you familiar with this story know Sidney claims to be a wizard, but then you'd also know that he's prone to exaggeration and you can't believe much of what Sidney says. He makes terrible jokes and at times he may seem a bit crude, but I feel that he likes Axel, Molly and their son, Sid, and has a good heart, so he may not mean his lies to harm anyone.

In the first book in the Dragonslayer trilogy, Sidney helps Axel learn how to kill dragons. In the second book, he incubates and raises twin dragons, and he uses them with Axel in developing the bombing technique that gets rid of the blue men, the invaders of the kingdom, so he's an important character in the story. I kind of like him. He's inventive, sly, a loner, essentially kind and generous, but he's had a hard life and I feel I should forgive him his many faults.

He's an interesting character to work with but a hard one to control. Once he has a life on the pages of the first book, he kind of takes over and does what he wants to. I'd plan on him doing one thing and sometimes he just won't have it and does as he pleases. An example or two might help you understand how difficult he's been. In the first book, *Dragonslaying is For Dreamers,* my plan was to have him accompany Axel on his hunt for dragons. Sidney won't go. There was no way that I could write the story with him leaving his valley. It was only after much effort that I was able to get him to attend Axel's wedding at the end of the book.

In the second book, *Axel Meets the Blue Men,* I wanted Sidney to stay and help the dying king. I meant for Axel to return to Greenwater and get Molly and Sid and take them back to the valley Axel bought from Sidney. But Axel starts to feel bad that Sidney's alone and invites him to go to the valley with him and ride back with Marie, Axel's friend. Because he hates to travel, I had planned on Sidney refusing to leave the castle, claiming that there was too much to do, but he tells Axel that he'll go with him.

I'm glad I found this record he started, and, as you will see, he certainly remains headstrong.

A RECENT HISTORY OF THE KINGDOM

As painful as it is to write with my old fingers, I'll fill as many pages as I can before I pass on. It's hard to know where to start. I don't know how much of my history you know. If you're familiar with Axel and his son, Sid, and the dragons that I helped Axel kill and the two I raised from an egg that Axel found and made me keep, then you know most of what's important.

You probably know Axel named his son after me. I like that. You remember that King Willard got sick just after the blue men were chased back into the sea with a plan I came up with to drop rotten dragon eggs on them. Axel had a small part in that. I like to give him credit when I can. If I want to keep my job as Court Wizard, I have to be careful what I say.

This has been an interesting part of my life, and there doesn't seem to be an end to the problems. No sooner do I solve one than another jumps up. The really bad times started ten or twelve years ago with an infestation of dragons. There were so many that the kingdom was being destroyed. When they'd taken most of the livestock, they started on people. Farming and trade stopped and everyone stayed indoors as much as they could.

Of course I knew all about this and was just waiting for the right person to come along and do all the things I no longer could. That's when I met Axel. He came to my valley one day looking for lessons in dragon killing. I taught him as much as he could learn in the short time I had and sent him off to help the king.

He didn't do a bad job of it either. Of course, most anyone could have with what I taught him. He even brought me back a dragon's egg. I didn't want to, but I felt I had to raise the two dragons that hatched from the double-yoked egg, and then I used them to save the kingdom a second time. That may sound like I'm taking all the credit, but I am a wizard and there isn't much I can't do, so I don't make a practice of being overly modest. I don't feel it's good to be extreme in anything.

If you didn't know all this before, you do now, and I can go on with the story from the time I got the king to make Axel a prince. That's close enough to what happened to make no difference. Of course Axel has new problems. I'll probably live long enough to save the kingdom one last time. This gets tiresome when you get older like I am. What I really like is taking naps. Every time I pass a soft-looking place, that's what I think of.

I thought most of the problems were about over when I escorted Axel and Rotug back to my valley. Rotug's the barbarian who helped me drive off the other blue men. Axel didn't want to leave him at Willardville because he didn't know our language yet, so Axel took him home to teach him. I let Axel and Molly live in my valley with my namesake and the stock I gave them.

I'm thinking of restocking the valley with chickens. Ought to make a nice retirement ranch once I get it fixed up like it was before I let Axel borrow it.

But, the king got sick and I knew he was at the end of his life and Axel would be king. That's hard to believe, even for me, but King Willard did make Axel a prince by adopting him after I told him that Axel helped me figure out how to get rid of the barbarians.

I should probably start this story with a description of how hard life is for a wizard. If you've never

That's all I found except for some light-colored stains and smears where someone had tried to clean something off some of the pages, and there were a few white feathers in among a small pile of rotted and bug-chewed pieces of paper. You may have missed some of the early and interesting parts of this story, but of course I know most of it so you shouldn't have any trouble catching up.

1

Patterns of sunlight, moving with the darker shadows that slid along the eastern maple-covered slopes made bright yellow patches that were dotted with the dull red of oaks and the dark green of the few pines. The cold wind that pushed the low clouds along the ridges created ripples in the colors as the trees swayed on the sides of the rounded mountains.

Axel and Rotug had spent most of the morning splitting logs they'd dragged from the hills and cut into lengths for burning. The yard next to the house smelled of freshly cut wood: the resiny tang of pine and the darker musk of oak.

It was a pleasure for Axel to watch Rotug using an axe for something other than a weapon. It took only one swing of the blade for the huge man to split all but the thickest logs. Axel had been alarmed when he had first given Rotug the axe and explained what he wanted him to do with it. Rotug had taken it by the handle and laughed as he hefted it. His laugh was as big as he was. He threw back his head and, opening his mouth wide exposing large irregular teeth, roared. His long blond hair shook but his stomach stayed firm and muscled. Then, one-handed and with little effort, had lifted the axe high and split a large log. He had turned and looked at Axel and with a smile said, "Good, yes?"

It had been a little more than a year ago that Axel's two friends had come back to the valley with him: Sidney, the wizard, who had helped Axel understand enough about dragons so he could blow them up with flaming arrows, and Rotug, one of the blue men who had chosen to stay when the rest of the barbarians were driven from the kingdom. Sidney had stayed for just two days, then with Marie had returned to Amory, King Willard's castle in Willardville. Rotug had stayed in the valley with Axel, Molly and their ten-year-old son, Sid. The large man had learned enough of their language that now he could communicate fairly well in simple sentences. The three of them had helped the barbarian learn the words for objects and how to ask for them and talk about them. Molly had enjoyed the teaching and was more patient with him than were Axel and Sid.

Axel and Sidney had told Molly all about their adventures at the castle and how they had come into possession of the large and gentle man, and at first she hadn't wanted to be alone or even to be near Rotug, but soon learned to trust him. Now Molly encouraged Rotug to take walks into the hills with her son. She knew that the stranger would die before he let anything bad happen to any of them.

Molly had had trouble believing Axel when he had told her about being adopted by the king and that he was now a prince. She had tossed her long, light-colored hair and laughed when Axel had told her about the dinner and how the king had told all his guests that he had always wanted a son and knew that he never would have one. How he had put his hand on Axel's shoulder and explained that he was adopting Axel and that Axel would be the next king.

She had been sure that the two men were playing a joke on her and had pretended to believe them, but finally they had convinced her that it was true, and so she had come to accept being married to a prince and that some-day Axel would be the king and she'd be the queen. It was a story to her, and she wasn't at all sure that she liked the idea. Axel acted like he hadn't had a choice, and Sidney sounded like he thought that it was a great opportunity for all of them.

The logs they were splitting were dry for the trees had been cut last winter, and the wood split cleanly with sharp pops when the blade bit into them. Axel was piling the pieces in the woodshed attached to the side of the house. Both men were warm and had removed their cloaks, but their breath puffed white in the cold air.

Four geese honked as they flew over the low hills on the far side of their small lake, lying misty and gray in the center of the valley. An answering call from the surface and the four, still in formation, banked as they circled, wheeling around the near shore to face the light breeze. After lowering their legs and spreading their wings against the air, they set their feet on the water and skidded to a stop near those hidden by mist. Axel looked up when he heard the light splashing as they hit.

Still facing the water, he said to Rotug, "We finish this load and do one more and we've got enough for the winter, Rotug."

Rotug turned and looked over his huge shoulder at Axel, and, after studying his slim but powerful body, set a new log on end and grinned as he said, "Axel tired?"

"Sure I am. You've kept me hopping this morning. What's the hurry?"

Rotug thunked the blade into the top of a log and turned to face his friend. Pushing his long blond hair away from his face, he said, "Messenger say king be sick and you go to castle to see. . .one growing year ago. You said we go to king when he say. I have. . .trouble waiting. When we can leave?"

Axel shook his head and grinned when he said, "I didn't say anything about 'we'."

Wiping his arm across his forehead, Rotug said, "You do. When we came to valley you say we all go back and see king when he say."

Axel cocked his head to one side and said, "It's been a while, but you're right, Rotug. I said that. But I'm not sure it's necessary for you to go, and there has to be somebody here to take care of my family and the farm."

"We leave now," Rotug said, gesturing toward the small barn. "Molly and Sid go, too. We be sure cow have hay, fix water so it go in tank and no freeze, leave grain sacks for chickens. What you think?"

Axel shook his head. "You have this all figured out so you must really want to go, eh?"

"Sure I do. I see you be king."

Axel sat on an upended log and said, "I doubt that'll happen, Rotug."

Rotug twisted the axe free and said, "I have this and next load split by night if I keep you at work."

Axel laughed and said, "If I wanted to I could stack this wood so fast I'd have to stand here waiting for you."

"We see," Rotug said as he attacked the logs, and the split pieces quickly began to pile up on either side of him.

Axel watched with pride as Rotug worked. He hadn't known if it would be a good idea bringing the huge, blond and full bearded man home with him. He hadn't known how Molly would feel about it, or even if she'd let him stay. Axel had explained to her that if Rotug hadn't come home with him he'd have had to stay in the castle, and he couldn't talk well enough for that yet. The soldiers might realize that he'd been one of the blue men and kill him. This had been the only real way to help him. Molly had said he could stay if they built a room in the barn for him to live and sleep in.

Axel hurried to the growing pile of firewood near the splitting stump, and, taking an armload at a time, ran to the shed and stacked it. In five trips he had the ground clean around the large man. He sat on the ground and smiled.

Rotug stopped working and rested the axe against the stump and, looking down at Axel, said, "You trick me, Axel."

"I did not. What are you talking about?" Axel said loudly.

"I see you throw wood behind over those logs when I not looking." Rotug grinned at Axel and continued as he palmed the sweat from his face. "Rotug find bunches and pieces back there."

"You sure about that?"

"I split and stack wood if wrong."

"For the whole winter?"

Rotug started for the pile to look and said, "The loser cut and stack wood for winter."

Axel smiled and said, "Done."

Rotug walked behind the pile of logs and in a moment came back, frowning. "What you do?"

"With what?"

"Wood you put back of pile."

Axel crossed his arms and asked, "Are you sure about what you saw?"

Rotug stood close to Axel and, looking down at him, said in a mock-cross voice, "Did you trick?"

"How could I have if there weren't any pieces back there?"

"You could," Here Rotug struggled for the word, "play trick. . .and, not tricking, be tricking."

Axel shook his head and said, "That's all very confusing and I'm getting hungry." He turned toward the house and said, "It must be lunch time."

There was still much about life in the kingdom that Rotug didn't understand, but he did trust Axel and he accepted almost all of what he and Molly told him. It had been just recently that Axel felt Rotug understood enough of the language for him to accept a light kidding. The first time Axel had tried to kid the huge man, he felt a fool, for Rotug just stood there and looked down at him. Axel hadn't tried a joke again for almost six months.

Rotug laughed with Axel as they washed at the well. Rotug was at least two feet taller than Axel and almost a foot wider. His arms and chest were huge and muscles rippled under his skin when he splashed water over his face and upper body.

Even though the water was cold enough to sting their hot skin, it felt good to wash away the dust and sweat of the morning. As Rotug was wiping the water from his arms, he said, "Men from castle call you Axel Prince, yes?"

"That's what they called me," Axel said as he wiped his thin face on the rough, gray fabric of his cloak.

"At castle they think you king someday?"

"I'm not sure. I think that's what King Willard had in mind when he adopted me." Axel ran his fingers through his damp hair and retied it behind his head as he continued. "Anyway, it won't be until the king dies."

"You say king sick when we leave."

Axel stopped moving and turned to Rotug and said, "That was over a year ago, Rotug." He watched as the huge man fastened his cloak. "A lot could have happened since then. He might have changed his mind about adopting me, or he could even have let his brother take over the kingdom."

When the two men entered the house, Sid was setting tin plates on the table, and Molly was near the sink cutting up a chicken she had broiled in the fireplace. After the clean, crispness of the early fall morning air, the one room building's wood smoke and cooked meat smell was a welcome change. When he saw his wife and son together like this, Axel was surprised but always pleased at how much they resembled each other. Sid was a good bit shorter than his mother, with the same light brown hair but with green eyes like his. Both their faces were long and oval shaped, and they moved their slender hands and fingers with the same gentle grace.

Rotug reached out a hand that was as large as Sid's head and snatched a piece of chicken from the cutting board, and, putting it in his mouth, said to Sid, "You ready go see king?"

Sid smiled when he looked up at the big man and said, "And the castle and all the knights and the towns that we'll have to go through. I'm ready to go right now." He turned to his father and asked, "When do we leave?"

Axel sat at the table and said, "I'm not sure. Rotug and I'll start in the morning, but I think it'd be best if you stayed here and protected your mother." Axel watched Molly's strong but still-slender back as he spoke.

Sid looked intently at his father and said, "You wouldn't leave me here, would you?"

"It could be dangerous, Sid. We don't know if the king's really dying or not. We just know what those

7

messengers said yesterday. It might be a plot. You remember the king has a brother?"

When Sid answered his voice had lost its eagerness. "Sure, I remember that but I don't remember his name."

"Rohn. He wants the kingdom. Must be a younger brother."

Sid drank water to wash some chicken down and said, "That doesn't sound like a problem. King Willard named you prince so you get to be the next king. The brother should know that."

Axel leaned forward and held his hands out to the sides of his plate and said, "It's clear to us, but we don't have royal blood and kings are supposed to."

Molly had stopped moving and was carefully watching this conversation, her head turning as the members of her family spoke. She gathered her long gray skirt about her legs as she sat at the table and said, "But you were adopted into the royal family by the king. That makes you royal, doesn't it?"

Axel was putting pieces of chicken on plates when he nodded at Molly and said to his son, "One thing you can't count on when someone dies, Sid, and that's that people will act reasonably. Greed gets in the way of their thinking almost every time. We can't plan on Rohn being reasonable about my being adopted. He might think that that's just a story and ignore it." Axel shrugged. "He might have a good argument, too."

"What can he do?" Sid asked, as he sat at his place at the small table across from his father.

"He's a powerful man, Sid. He has a castle, lands, and his own knights, and from what I heard, he's got an army. That's why I don't want you in the middle of it all."

"If it's that dangerous you shouldn't go alone," Sid said.

"I made promises to the king so I've got to go." Axel's voice hardened, "You don't."

Sid took the very serious tone with his voice that only children can have while talking with their parents, and said, "You're my father and that's more important to me than you being a prince is to you. So, if it's important that you go, it's even more important for me that I go along so I can help."

Axel glanced at his wife and caught her soft lips smiling as she off broke off large pieces of fresh bread, still hot from the box oven built onto the right side of the fireplace. The steam gushed from the broken loaf and the yeasty smell hung over the table.

This sounded like the argument he'd had with her years ago when he was called the first time to the castle to help the king. Molly must have recognized it, too, and that's what had made her smile.

At that time he had felt that he should go and Molly hadn't wanted him to. In his mind he heard again that conversation with Molly's sweet and reasonable voice as she urged him to stay home when she said:

"You can't go and fight in a war we don't know anything about."

"If there was an invasion and everybody said that, then nobody would show up and the invaders would take over."

"If everybody else stayed home, you'd be stupid to go. You'd be the only one there."

Axel remembered shaking his head and saying, *"But that's not the way it is. Everyone who cares about the kingdom will go to help."*

"Let them. If they all go, then whether you go or not won't make any difference, will it?"

Axel sat quietly for a moment, then shook his head and said, "Sid, when you're finished with lunch, why don't you catch some fish and we'll eat them tonight? We'll talk about this then. Rotug has to finish splitting wood, and I might just sit on a log and watch him work."

2

Sid swung the line back and forth on the end of the slender branch his father had fashioned into a fishing pole. He lowered his arm, and the hook and piece of wood he used for a bobber splashed lightly. After finding a place on the bank to sit, he held the pole steady and watched the small piece of wood as it slowly rose and fell on the gently moving but smooth surface.

Glancing up when he heard a short honk of alarm, he saw two geese running on the water to gain speed then slowly rising from the small lake. They trailed strings of droplets which shone silver in the sunlight. His dog, Grrr, stood when the geese cried and watched as they banked and flew low over the valley then into the yellowed hills.

When he turned back, Sid saw movement in the tree line on the far side of the lake. Two men on horses rode out of the shadows and into the sunlight. Though strangers were rare in their valley, the boy was not concerned, for the men rode slowly and one waved in a friendly way when they reached the opposite shore. Grrr took his lead from Sid and was alert but didn't stand or give warning as he would have if he'd seen the men as a threat.

Sid watched them as they rode around the lake and halted their horses near the bank next to him and Grrr. The large dog now stood, the hair stiff on his back, and moved between the men and the boy. Sid could hear the low rumbling of his warning growl and put his hand on the dog's dark brown back to steady him.

The darker of the two men, the one with the full beard and dark eyes, brushed dust from his undyed cloak and dark pants when they had dismounted, and asked gently, "How's fishing?"

"Nothing yet," Sid replied, as Grrr moved toward the men, his legs stiff and his tail held straight up.

"Hold off your dog. We mean you no harm," said the second, smaller man as he moved closer. He was dressed much the same way, and his long, hawk-like nose dominated his thin face. Sid could see he was smiling with tight lips for he was clean shaven, and he kept his small eyes on the dog.

Grrr was now in his full protective stance and his growl was loud and clear.

"What do you want? My father's over there," Sid said, pointing behind him toward the house, a small one-story building with a low barn behind it.

After looking at the house for a moment, the bearded man asked, "What's your father's name?"

Sid didn't think he should talk to these strangers, but there couldn't be harm in telling them who his father was. Besides, he was proud of his father. He spoke loudly when he said, "Sir Axel."

The smaller man glanced toward his companion, who nodded slightly, then toward the house. Taking a short step, he leaned over Grrr and grabbed Sid by the upper arm and pulled him to his feet. Grrr lunged and clamped hard on the man's arm, and Sid could hear a bone snap as the dog put his weight on the hold. Crying out and pulling back, the man let go of Sid and jerked a knife from his belt. He slashed at the dog, putting a cut across his ribs on the left side.

Sid yelled, "Don't hurt my dog," and leaning down to do so, sank his teeth into the back of the hand that held the knife and bit down as hard as he could. He felt the small bones crack and tasted blood.

The man now had the large brown dog hanging from one arm and Sid hanging from his other hand. He screamed in rage; and his companion, now standing by his horse, ran to the struggle and sank the toe of his boot deeply into Grrr's side. The dog let go of the arm, and with a whoof of air, collapsed to the ground. The large man then jerked on Sid until the boy couldn't hold on with his teeth any longer, then pulled him away from his companion and clamped his hand over the boy's mouth. He held Sid with one arm and, after dragging him to his horse, with some difficulty swung with him into the saddle and said in a low voice, "Let's go."

The wounded man took his cut hand from his mouth and said, "Wait. The message." He ran to his horse and, fumbling with the straps on a pack behind the saddle until he could open it, pulled out a rolled piece of stiff paper. Looking up at the mounted man, he said, "Where?"

"There by the boy's fishing pole," his companion said and pointed to the bank where Sid had been sitting.

Holding his arm against his side, he put the now bloody paper under the pole and ran back to his horse. Grrr was standing but was too hurt to follow as the two horses galloped around the lake and into the woods on its far side.

3

Two hours later, the men were again sweating heavily but had most of the pile of logs split. After looking up, Rotug pointed to the lake and said, "That Grrr?"

Axel stopped picking up wood, looked and said, "Yes." He watched the dog's slow progress toward them and said, "But there's something wrong with him." He threw the log he was holding aside and ran toward the dog, who was just rounding the near side of the lake and limping badly. When the men reached him, he lay in the dried grasses, whimpering.

Axel knelt next to Grrr, and, in the musk and coppery smell, examined a deep cut that exposed a line of dark red, blood-covered ribs. Rotug was looking toward the lake, his hand shading his eyes from the afternoon sun. "I no see Sid. Where he fishing?"

Axel was examining the cut but looked up, "What?"

"Where Sid?"

Axel jumped to his feet and faced the lake. "He fishes on the far side by that row of bushes." He, too, shaded his eyes and both men looked carefully around the shore of the lake. Axel turned toward the house and yelled, "Molly." When she came to the doorway, Axel pointed at Grrr and said, "Take care of Grrr." Then both men ran toward the line of bushes, Rotug following closely behind Axel. The men ran through the weeds, long grasses and cattails that grew alone the shore, sometimes jumping over patches of water and sometimes splashing through them.

It was on the far shore that they found Sid's fishing pole lying in the sand next to a large rock holding down a short rope leading into the water with one fish strung on it. They both turned and looked at the nearest tree line.

"He gone."

"I can see that."

"Yes. What we do?"

"We find him." Axel's eyes skimmed the surface of the small lake. "He wouldn't be in the water, it's too cold for swimming. He wouldn't have wandered off, he left a fish tied here in the shallows. Somebody's got him and they had to hurt Grrr to do it. Help me look for tracks."

It was then that Axel spotted the piece of paper weighted down by the fishing pole. He picked it up, and as he unrolled it, noticed the blood. He fingers shook as he read aloud. "We have the boy. He will be released. Do not come to Amory. Do not try to take over the kingdom. Do not try to find the boy. If you do he will die."

Axel silently read the note a second time and then again. The words didn't change. They sounded hollow in his head. Someone had taken Sid. Someone who didn't want him to claim the throne. It had to be the king's brother or one of his people. Axel could feel the blood rushing to his face, and yet his arms felt numb. There was a wind sound that closed his ears and his hands were so weak that he almost dropped the paper. He noticed then the hoof prints and scuffed ground.

Axel tried two times before he could speak, "It looks like there were two of them on horses. Rotug, you follow these tracks while I get horses, my sword and your axe." Axel turned and ran toward the house and Molly.

4

Axel and Rotug followed the tracks until it grew too dark and made camp for the night by a creek. Axel tried to eat some of the food Molly had pushed toward him as he was running out the door, but he couldn't force the bread down. Rotug had no trouble eating, but he kept his eyes on Axel, for he was as worried about Sid. He had grown to like him almost as he might a younger brother.

In the morning, Axel and Rotug were up as soon as it was light enough to see the ground. The morning sky was clear but cold looking and the air was brittle with the smell and feel of coming snow. Their breath made small clouds around their heads when they talked.

Rotug was good at reading any sign left in the soft ground and leaves. They followed the scuff marks and hoof prints east, higher into the mountains. Rotug ran along the path, bent at the waist, his face turned toward the ground. Axel rode, leading Rotug's horse behind his.

By noon of the second day they were following the marks up the steep trail, and, when they were near the crest of one of the lower peaks, they lost them in the rocks. Soon the trail split into three paths, each going a separate direction,

Rotug dropped to his knees to look for sign. Axel dismounted and tied the horses to a low limb and knelt next to the giant and watched him as he studied the ground. The dampness of the stirred leaves and moss rose to him when Rotug brushed aside debris to look at the bare ground. He would then press his fingers into depressions in the dirt or leaves and hold them there a second, and then grunt and remove them. Axel couldn't tell what he was looking for but had confidence that Rotug knew what he was doing.

Rotug examined carefully all three paths. The split came just as the trail left the soft ground and led into shelves of rock which were still wet in shady places and in the shadows were covered in silver moss.

There were some scuff marks on the stone, but Rotug ignored them. Axel felt maybe he could tell that they were old or didn't mean anything. Certainly deer, wild pigs and bears used the trail. He had seen the dried evidence of their passing, and some of the trees had claw marks higher than a man's head running down their trunks. He didn't know how Rotug could tell one scuff mark from another, but he trusted him.

Rotug rose from his knees and, looking at Axel, shook his head as he said, "Trail hard to see."

Axel turned and looked to the west, back toward their valley. The mist still hung on the sides of the mountains like smoke from fires. He was torn between an intense desire to charge ahead in any direction, looking for his son, and returning to their farm and Molly. There wasn't any choice for Axel to make, for he couldn't leave Molly alone with a wounded dog for protection while he rode off, maybe never to come back. They had one chance in three of guessing right and those weren't good odds.

Axel hated to but had to admit to himself that Sid was lost to them for now. They could never follow the two horses fast enough to catch up with them. Axel told Rotug to continue following the tracks and mark his trail with signs. He would return for Molly and they'd catch up to him.

5

Molly, her hands to either side of her face and her heart beating heavily in her chest, had watched the two men disappear into the trees at the foot of the hills. Rotug rode their plow horse, and Axel, the huge white warhorse the king had given him. She turned, stooped and began to examine Grrr's side with her gentle fingers.

"This looks like it hurts, Grrr. I'll have to sew it up, and with rest, you'll feel better in a short while," she said through the catches in her chest as the sobbing slowed. She was able to coax Grrr to the doorway of the house and there he lay, his eyes half closed. "That cut shouldn't make you feel so bad. You must have some hurt I can't see." She ran her fingers gently through the dog's dirty coat. When she touched his side, Grrr tensed and his head turned so he could look at her. Molly ran her hand softly over the dog's head and said, "You lie there and I'll at least get your cut fixed."

With her sewing materials from the house next to her, Molly carefully washed Grrr's side, then, with one of her smallest needles, sewed the flaps of skin together. Grrr whimpered when she did this, but he must have known that she was helping him for he didn't move.

When she had done all she could for the dog, Molly went into the house and began to prepare food and pack for her trip. If Axel didn't come back by the next day, she was going to follow him. She couldn't sit here and not know what was going on.

6

Molly was relieved when she saw Axel round the lake after he had returned to the valley, and she stepped out of the house and waved her arms. She knew that Sid was sitting behind Axel on his horse. She just couldn't see him yet. . .but she could see him in her mind. He'd be holding onto Axel's saddle, and he'd have a smile on his face, for he was back home in his valley with his parents. He had to be there. She started running toward the lake and her family.

Axel felt awful. This is the first time he had failed his wife and it had to be with Sid. What could he have done differently? Should he have refused to let King Willard adopt him? Then there would be no reason for anybody to kidnap Sid. But, how was he to know? He hadn't refused because that's what the king wanted and he was a knight and had to do what the king asked of him, and he had wanted to help the king. Once again duty had gotten in the way of desire.

When they were close enough that she could see that there weren't any little boots sticking out on either side of Axel's saddle, Molly stopped running. She stood in the grass at the edge of the meadow and held her arms to her chest. Bile rose in her throat so that she could taste it, yet she felt hollow and empty. She had no insides to hold her up. The sky got dark and turned so that the clouds moved and spun in the sky. She could feel her legs give way and then the grass pushed against the side of her face.

Axel dismounted and held Molly close to his chest until she regained consciousness. The welcome smell of her hair as it brushed against his face comforted him. "We'll find him, Molly. We'll do what has to be done.

We'll leave for the castle in the morning. We'll find him. We have to."

He rocked there in the grass with his wife in his arms until Molly struggled to sit and said, "Where is he, Axel? Where's my son?" Her eyes were running tears, and there was no answer Axel could give her to lessen the pain he knew she was feeling. It had to be much like his own. He held her tightly and said, "They won't harm him. That would do them no good. They just want to control me. He may be scared but he'll be all right."

Molly asked with hope in her voice, "How do you know that? He's just a baby."

"They don't want him, they just want to use him. They can't if he's dead, so they won't kill him, Molly."

The next morning was cold and the fields around the lake shone frost-silver in the sun as Axel packed Winthton and saddled the horses. Axel examined Grrr. He seemed much better. The wound in his side wasn't infected and he was moving easier. They weren't going to be traveling fast with Winthton, their donkey, so Grrr should be able to keep up with little trouble.

7

Axel and Molly caught up with Rotug on the trail. As the three travelers reached each new town, Axel was surprised that life appeared so normal, for they had been thoroughly ravaged by the blue men. Some of the burned farms had been rebuilt and their yards were free of the trash left by the invaders. In some places it was if there had been no invasion. He knew that there were scars on the people, though. You couldn't lose members of your family or even of your town and not have it change the way you felt and not remember it forever.

It was just a week after Sid had been taken that Axel, Molly and Rotug were looking down at the town of Willardville and past it to the solid walls and tall towers of Amory, King Willard's castle. The wind, always from the sea, was wet and had winter's sting to it. Dark clouds lay heavily over the water, and below them the rain fell in slanting, gray pillars. To the west squatted the Blue Mountains, their tops pushing up at the low and bulging clouds. Miles away, behind them, mostly covered by clouds, they could see just the base of the mountain that towered over the small town of Tightly.

Rotug wanted to stop and eat and let Grrr rest but Axel insisted that they push on. He couldn't think of anything but reaching the castle and getting help finding Sid, and he knew that Molly felt the same way. Rotug dismounted and unwrapped the food and began to eat. There was nothing that Axel and Molly could do but join him.

Earlier, they had rested at the base of the mountain near Tightly, sitting with their backs against the huge fallen slabs of stone imbedded in the ground as if they had been planted there ages ago. They had faced the sun and let it warm them. In the shade, the grass and weeds were still brittle and crisp with frozen dew, and they put a cloth down for Molly to sit on.

Axel had explained to Molly and Rotug that the huge, sharp-edged stones had fallen from the side of the mountain when winter rain had frozen in cracks and the expanding ice had broken the pieces from the face of the cliffs. Axel pointed out to Rotug that this was the cause of the mountain's flat-seeming sides.

He told about his climb to the third ledge and what the dragon had looked like, how surprised he'd been at its size and the smell of rotten meat that was so strong that he'd had to breathe through his mouth. Then he remembered that he'd had to keep his teeth tightly clamped together to keep out the dark green flies that swarmed over the edge, feeding on meat left on the bones.

Rotug asked, "Why you never tell about dragons, Axel? I ask."

Axel thought before he replied, "I never like to think about killing, and If I talked to you or anybody about it, I'd have to think about it." He was silent for so long that Rotug thought that he might be done talking about that part of his life, but Axel looked up at the ledges and continued. "It's been a long time, Rotug. Some of the feelings I had about killing are gone now. I think I can talk about it if you want me to."

"I do. You tell Sidney helped. What was that?"

Axel shifted his weight against the boulder as he scratched his back against the rough stone and was silent for a bit before he began speaking slowly. He was stroking Grrr's head as he said, "I met Sidney when I first started out, when I thought that if I could just kill a dragon, I'd make lots of money." Axel laughed at himself, and turning toward his wife, continued. "A dumb idea, but that's the kind of thinking I did then.

"Sidney read to me about dragons out of some old books he had, and we figured out that if I could get fire into their mouths just as they were taking in air to shoot out flame, they might suck the fire into their stomachs and burn up."

Rotug was chewing a hard crust of bread while closely watching Axel's face. "Did that way work like that? Dragons burn?"

Axel saw again a flaming arrow sinking deep into a dark green throat and the flame being drawn down past a long, black, snake-like tongue. "No, not exactly." Now he heard the cries of the small female as she struggled against the hook that held her in the chimney, her claws cutting and scraping on the stone and her wings beating the walls of her prison. He saw her yellow eyes with their thin, black slits staring at him with hatred and frustration. He again shot an arrow up the chimney into her screaming mouth. Axel shook his head to get rid of the images and smiled at Molly.

"Not really, Rotug. They exploded."

"What mean, 'exploded'?"

How to describe it? Axel held his hands together and quickly spread his fingers apart as he said, "Like this." Axel could tell that Rotug didn't understand what he was showing him and went on. "You know what an egg does when it's boiled too long? It breaks apart and the insides come out?"

Rotug smiled and said, "Sure, you cook that way."

Axel nodded at him and said, "It was like that, only it happened all at once. Really quick."

23

"Dragon came apart like egg?"

"No. They blew apart and the pieces flew all over."

"Why?"

This was complicated. "Sidney read to me about their stomachs. They have more than one you know, and one of them holds their food as it rots. That happens to be the stomach they store the gas in so they can shoot fire."

"Why they blow up?"

Axel didn't really know. "We figured out that if I could get fire into their mouths just as they were taking air into that gas stomach, they'd burn up. They blew up instead."

Molly stopped eating and said, "Axel, that's disgusting talk while we're eating"

Rotug was watching Axel closely now, fascinated by this story. He said, "You scared?"

Axel laughed and settled back on the grass and said, "Was I ever scared. I was so scared when I shot that first dragon that I didn't think I could move."

"Why you no run?"

Axel looked at the sun shining on his friend's face and said "If I had, you wouldn't be here now."

"Where I be at?"

"You would have been killed at the castle. He shook his head. "Let's pack up and go."

Rotug didn't stand when Axel did, and Axel, surprised, turned and looked down at him. The giant said, "All dragons have gas stomach?"

"I suppose so."

"Twin dragons?"

"Sure. Why?"

"I just ask, Axel."

8

They had stopped on the hill just south of Willardville and Axel and Molly were talking about how he was going to present himself to the king and his knights. Axel didn't know anything about the situation here beyond the king sending for him to come. Years ago, at the time the king had adopted him, he had promised that he'd come to the castle any time the king sent for him. He had refused to stay in Amory as the king asked, and much to his relief, the king had allowed him to return to his family and live in their valley near Greenwater. Axel and the king had come to an understanding. Since the king was sick and might die soon, that when Axel was needed at the castle, he'd come.

Axel pulled his cloak closer to cut out the cold mist and pointed to the spine of land that left the road and twisted up to the castle's tall gate. The heavy door was lowered, so the bridge over the moat was in place, but there were few people moving to or from the castle.

The mist and fog that rose from the sea and flowed over the lip of the cliff smelled coldly of salt and dead fish. The fog rose up the sides of the castle so that most of the lower floors were shrouded in gray. Molly could just see the drawbridge when Axel pointed it out. "That's the only way into the castle that most people know about, Molly. Impressive, isn't it?"

When Molly patted her horse on the neck to quiet it, she left her hand on the welcome warmth and said, "I knew it was big because you told me it was, but I had no idea it would be like this. That's the tallest building there ever could be. No one could ever get in there. I don't know what the king needs you for. He has all the protection anyone could ever want."

Axel checked for Grrr and saw him hunting mice in the frosted grass at the side of the road and knew he was almost his old self. When the large dog smelled or heard a mouse moving in the brittle grass, he'd stand still and wait to be sure where it was, then pounce with both front feet. He was getting good at this for he usually came up with a small rodent in his mouth. One crunch and it was gone.

Axel urged his horse forward as he said, "I don't know either and it's cold up here. Let's go down, find Sidney and get next to a fire. He can tell us what's going on if anyone can."

The moat had been created by cutting into the spine of rock that carried the road from the town to the castle. When the three crossed over the moat on the heavy door that had been lowered to become a bridge, their horse's hooves clattered on the hard wood and echoed from the rocks far below.

Axel didn't expect the guard to recognize him, and of course, he didn't. The man stood in the middle of the tall doorway, his halberd held across his chest and looked up at Axel and said, "Halt there, strangers. What business you got in Amory?"

Axel's white war horse had led the way to the gate and the two plow horses leading Winthton followed, and, when Axel stopped, the three horses were standing side by side with Winthton behind them. Grrr was on guard next to Axel's horse.

Molly had only to shift her eyes to glance at her husband and noticed that Axel didn't look down at the guard which surprised her. She had expected him to ask to enter the castle, but Axel looked straight ahead and said, "I am Prince Axel. Call a stableboy to care for our horses. They need oats, water and a good brushing. The same for the donkey. And his pack should be taken off. The dog will remain with us."

Still looking through the gate and into the courtyard, and not waiting for the man to answer, Axel urged his horse forward, and the guard stepped aside. Molly, looking forward herself now, followed him into the nearly empty courtyard. She looked at Axel as she never had before. He seemed sure of himself and was sitting so tall in the big war saddle that she almost didn't know him. He's acting like he's king already, she thought.

They dismounted near the archway into the great room and, sure enough, there was a stableboy waiting to take their horses. The boy was surprised that this man had asked for oats for a donkey, but if that's what he was ordered to give it, he would.

Molly was amazed by the size of the courtyard and the stalls where there were people at work. Axel had described the castle in detail to her many times. She had insisted on the telling and retelling. She wanted to hear it over and over again. Now she was here. It would be wonderful if only she wasn't so worried about Sid. She could think about the castle only in terms of the help they might get here in finding her son.

Axel explained to Molly what they were seeing as they entered each room. She was as surprised as Axel had been the first time he had come to the castle. It was the size of the rooms, both the distance to the far walls and the high ceilings that were the most amazing.

Axel led the way into the great hall and through the low doorway into the king's kitchen, saying as he did so,

"Watch your head, Rotug." Turning and looking back as the huge man stepped through the doorway, he saw Rotug bang his forehead against the stones of the arch. He held his head with his hands and asked Molly, "How I see own head?"

Molly was more comfortable in the smoky kitchen, for here the dark beams hung low and the room was cramped, hot and filled with smoke and cooking odors. The walls were lined with bags of what looked like potatoes and onions or beets. Large earthenware jars filled the shelves on the wall to the right of the stove, and on the other side squatted a stone sink. In the center of the room there was a long table with benches on either side.

A fat woman standing by the table with her hands on her hips looked closely at them as they entered. She wore a long apron that had once been white, but now was covered in old food stains where the fat rolls on her body had pushed it out in smooth billows. Her round head was cocked to the side and rested on one shoulder, as if her neck had been broken.

Her voice was hoarse and aggressive when she said, "What ya want here? I'm not feeding no travelers, so ya might as well go on about yer business." When Grrr stepped around Axel and into the dim light, she said, "And get that dog out of here with you."

Axel was looking into the dark corners of the smokey room as he asked, "Where's Orna?"

The fat woman laughed and said, "That old thing. She hasn't been here for months. Where you know her from?"

Axel, talking in a stern voice Molly hadn't heard before, said, "I'm Prince Axel, and you'll do yourself a favor to keep a civil tongue, woman. Now, what's your name?"

The cook glanced from Axel to the blond giant next to him then at Molly and wiped her hands on her stained apron and asked, "Who?"

"You."

"Prince of what?"

"Do you know a wizard called Sidney?"

"Oh, him. Everybody knows that old fake and his stupid chicken." She looked up at Axel through slitted eyes and asked, "Why? He a friend of yours?"

"Where is he?"

Her voice took on a crafty edge now as she said, "I don't know if he wants me to tell you. There's been lots of funny things going on around here lately, and I don't wanna say more than I already have." When she got no response, she expected them to leave, and when they didn't, she turned and began washing a large pot at the stone sink. Axel gestured for Rotug and Molly to sit at the table with him. "How about something to eat? Orna always had something good around for hungry travelers."

The cook turned and said, "Prince of what?"

Molly spoke for the first time and now adopted Axel's new stronger attitude, "My husband's going to be the next king."

Axel reached across the narrow table and put his hand on her arm to silence her and said, "I was friends with Orna and we'd like to be friends with you, too. Could we begin again?"

The woman crossed the small room and stood by the table looking down at Axel and said, "Sure. What's this about being king? And if that's true, what ya doing in the kitchen? Kings and such call for food in the great room or in their rooms. Kings don't come in here asking for scraps like beggars."

Axel laughed and said in a much softer way, "I don't have much practice at being royal yet. I'm still learning how to act. Maybe you could help. . . . Would you do that?"

The woman put her hands on the table top and lowered her fat body down on the bench next to Molly and let out a long sigh. When she had settled on the bench like a balloon would if filled with water, she said, "I guess I could. I've only lived here in the castle about half a year, but there's not much that goes on I don't know about. But first, you got to tell me who you are and what this talk about being a king's all about. You don't act like any king I ever saw."

Axel saw Rotug shift his weight and thought he might be going to say something so he shook his head slightly while looking into the giant's blue eyes. Rotug relaxed.

Axel's tone changed and he also acted much more relaxed as he said, "That's kind of you. What's your name?"

The fat woman hesitated, then said, "They call me Cook now."

"What did they call you before you became a cook?"

"You."

"What?"

"You."

Axel glanced at Molly then back at the cook and said again, "What did they call you?"

"I just told you. Can't you hear right?"

Axel smiled, glanced down at the scarred top of the table and then up again and said, "You? They called you 'You'?"

"That's what they called me, You. Sometimes, If I didn't move fast enough or something, they called me Hey, You."

"What did your mother call you?"

"Girl."

Molly and Axel looked at each other for a moment. Molly smiled slightly and said, "What do you want us to call you?"

Now the fat woman smiled and her eyes disappeared into her face as she said, "I got enough to do without you calling me anything."

Axel laughed loudly and the air in the dark kitchen seemed to lighten and the woman relaxed. When he had settled down, Axel asked, "About that food?"

The woman put her palms on the table and pushed herself upright, and breathing hard, said, "Just wait a bit and I'll have something. I can always give a man who laughs something to eat. Maybe even something for that big dog." As she turned away she said, "What you want with the wizard?"

"He's a friend of ours," Axel said.

She turned and asked. "How long you known him?"

"It seems like my whole life."

"And you're still friends?" She shook her head as she turned to put bread on a plate. "I can't think of anyone being friendly with Sidney that long."

9

A voice at the door shouted, "Who's talking about me?"

Axel jumped up and yelled, "Sidney."

Sidney, with his pet chicken on his shoulder, was wearing a new black cloak with silver stars and the moon on it, but already there were the white stains below the shoulders on both sides. His bald head was fringed by a thin line of white hair that was much longer than Axel remembered. But his round face still had no wrinkles and was smooth and pink.

When Sidney recognized the three people sitting at the table, he gave a short hop and spun around and danced a few steps as he sang out, "Axel, Molly and Rotug. I've never seen people I wanted to see more. Come here, Axel," He jumped up and down and held out his arms.

When Sidney yelled and moved quickly, Grrr charged forward and stood between Sidney and his family. The hair on his back was up and he was braced for an attack. When Axel said, "Down, Grrr," the dog relaxed and lay at Axel's feet.

Axel stood and the two men ran toward each other. And this time when Sidney moved quickly, Cynthia, his white chicken, squalled and fluttered to the table. The old cook waddled over with a meat cleaver and thunked it into the hard wood just short of the chicken's feet.

Sidney yelled, "Stop that," and he grabbed his pet and returned her to his left shoulder just before he and Axel started slapping each other on the back and acting like they hadn't seen each other in ten years instead of the one year it had been. They said things like: "You haven't changed one bit," and, "I'd know you anywhere," and, "How have you been?"

Molly watched fascinated with these greetings. She had never seen her husband act so excited before. She'd seen him greet other men when they'd stopped at their farm, but he hadn't acted this way.

When the celebrations were over, Sidney turned and looked at Molly, who was standing next to the table with a grin on her face. "Is this the beautiful Molly I know? You're getting younger and prettier every time I see you." Sidney reached out and hugged her and, being careful of Cynthia, she hugged him back as she laughed, the first time Axel had heard her laugh in days.

Next, Sidney slapped Rotug on the back and the huge man smiled and slapped Sidney's back as he had seen Axel do it. Sidney flew across the kitchen and only stopped himself from falling into the large sink by grabbing onto a post that was holding up the stove. When Sidney was standing by himself again, Rotug held him out at the length of his arms and studied his face. "You look like belong here, you barbarian you."

Sidney frowned then laughed. He turned to Axel and said, "It looks like you've civilized this blue monster. He can even talk now."

Rotug laughed and said, "I talk good. What you want I say?"

Sidney laughed and motioned for everyone to sit. Turning to the cook, he called out, "Woman, bring us food and drink. This is the next king so you better be quick about it."

10

Axel cleared his throat and sat at the table and said, "Sidney, what's been going on here? We got bad trouble and need to know everything you know about the situation with the king and Rohn."

Sidney shook his head and said, "You think you got troubles?" He held up fingers as he said, "One, the king's dying; two, Rohn has sent messages that he's going to take the throne. Half the serfs are so afraid that want to give it to him, and I can't blame them too much; three, Rohn's got a big army. At least three times as many men as we do."

He stopped talking and looked from one face to another, and when he saw that the three weren't interested in the troubles of the castle, asked, "What do you mean, you got trouble? What's yours?"

Axel glanced at Molly, took a breath and said all in a rush, "Someone took Sid."

Sidney leaned forward waiting for Axel to go on, but when he didn't, he looked first at Molly and then at Rotug. They, too, stared back and said nothing. The cook watched everyone as if they were snakes. Sidney said, "Go on, Axel, what happened?"

"That's all there is, Sidney. He was fishing and didn't come back with Grrr. We found this paper under his pole." Axel pulled the note from his pouch and leaned over the table as he handed it to Sidney.

Reading to himself, his lips forming the words, Sidney worked through the note twice and looked up at his friend. "This all you know?"

Tears were running down Molly's face but she didn't seem to notice them as she said, "You've got to help us,

Sidney. You're the only friend we've got. Tell us everything. Help us." She burst into sobs and now covered her
face with her hands and her shoulders shook. Axel put his
arm around her shoulders and held her as he looked at his
friend.

"I have axe tied to horse. Tell who took Sid. I kill.
Small piece I cut."

When Sidney turned to the huge man, he was surprised
to see that his eyes, too, were wet. He studied the top of
the table for a long time, looked up and said, "It has to
be Rohn. Nobody else would do it. The note says that you
aren't to come to the castle or try to take the kingdom.
Rohn would be the only one who would feel that way.
Here, everyone loves you, Axel. You saved the kingdom
from the barbarians and you're a hero to them, and they
expect you to be the king."

Rotug banged his big fist on the table and all four of
its legs jumped up and off the floor. "You tell Rotug
where is Rohn. I find Sid back."

Sidney held up his hands. "Wait a bit here. We can't
just go off and attack Rohn. He's in his castle. He has all
those men guarding him. He expects trouble and he wants
to be king." Sidney turned his palms out and continued,
"We have a problem here and we have to look at it as if
we really could solve it or we'll just make a mess of
everything."

Axel relaxed. These were familiar words to him. He
remembered when Sidney had said similar things when
they'd had problems in the past, and it had always worked
out. Sidney had a way of thinking through problems and
had taught Axel, but Axel had been so upset by his son's
capture that he hadn't been thinking clearly. Now he

could; he had Sidney to help him. "We'll have to talk about this, Sidney."

He turned to Molly and said, "Cook will show you what rooms we can have. Sidney and I have work to do. You go with Rotug. He'll show you around the castle. Or, you could take a nap. I know you must be tired."

Molly stood. "No. You can't get rid of me. I want to help." She then raised her voice and punctuated her words by jabbing her finger toward floor, "I'm staying right here and I'm going to be in on everything you two decide to do. Send Rotug to bed if you want to, but I'm part of any plan you're going to make." Molly sat again and crossed her arms over her chest, set her jaw and looked at Axel.

Molly had never talked like this before. This was a new experience for Axel and he didn't know what to say. Sidney did though. He said, "Molly, you're right. You have to be as upset as we are and you've a right to be in on the plans." He turned to Rotug and said, "Cook will show you your room. You can wait for us there."

Rotug looked at Axel then at Molly and said, "No, you no rid of me too. I worry for little Sid like rest of you. I stay with Molly and Axel and plan." He sat next to Molly.

Sidney slammed his small hand down on the table and said, "So be it." The sound and the shaking of the table was like a faint echo of when Rotug had done it, but this unexpected action was just as effective. The four leaned their heads toward each other to plan together what they could do.

Axel looked around the dark room, then said to Sidney, "How's the king? Is he really dying? Two messengers came to the valley and told me to come."

Sidney nodded and, leaning further across the narrow table, put his hand on Axel's shoulder and looked into his eyes and said, "The king's going fast, Axel. Are you prepared to be king in the next month or so?"

Molly and Axel said almost together, "So soon?"

Sidney nodded and said in a low voice, "I was the one who sent the messengers. He sleeps almost all the time now. He eats little and never gets out of bed. He's blind and he can't hear anything unless it's yelled into his left ear. I'm surprised he's lasted this long. I didn't think you'd get here in time." He glanced at Molly and continued, "Now tell me about Sid."

Molly said, "We told you everything. He just disappeared and Axel found that note. We didn't hear or see anything except some horse tracks that led east into the hills. Rotug lost them there when the trail split." She turned and looked at Axel and continued. "Axel came back and got me and we packed as fast as we could and caught up with Rotug.

"He was on foot and had been breaking branches pointing the way so we could follow him." She looked back at Sidney and continued in a much smaller voice, almost as if she, too, were surprised at the way she was speaking out, "That's how we found him. . .by the broken branches. . .on the trail," She hunched her shoulders and bent her head over the top of the table, and Axel could hear her crying.

Axel looked at the top of Molly's head and said, "Molly's right, that's all we know, Sidney. Now. . .you have to help us get Sid back. That's the first thing and all the rest of this can wait on that."

Putting his elbows on the table and spreading his hands to either side, Sidney said, "Sure, Axel, but where is he?

We can't just go off calling his name. He was taken by people with a plan. If we're going to get him back we have to have one, too."

Molly wiped her eyes with the palms of her hands, looked at Sidney and said, "Where does this Rohn have his castle? He has to be there."

Rotug had been watching each speaker and when Molly said this, he said, "Yes, Sid at castle with brother. That way bad brother can watch. We go to brother castle and get Sid back," He nodded his head as if the problem had been solved.

Sidney sat up straighter and said. "That's it. That's what we'll do, get the blue men to help us."

Molly clapped her hands together and with a smile on her face said, "Wonderful, Sidney. When can they start?"

"I haven't worked this out yet, Molly, I just thought of it. We'll have to plan this carefully. They're kind of wild and this has to be thought out precisely."

"What do you have in mind, Sidney?" Axel asked.

"I'm not sure. Let me talk this out with you. We have to list what we have and how it could help us." He worked with his fingers again. "One, we have Rotug." Rotug nodded and said, "Rotug help." Sidney went on, "Two, we have the blue men."

Axel interrupted him, "We don't have the blue men. We don't even know where they live, and we sure don't want to invite them here. They weren't much fun their first visit as I remember."

"That's how we use Rotug. He knows where they live. You don't know this because you haven't been here, Axel, but they did come back one time and they sent one blue man in a small boat to shore. He didn't have an axe with him and the king sent me down to the beach to see what he wanted."

Molly put her hand to her mouth and her eyes were very big. "Oh, Sidney, how brave."

Sidney smiled behind his hand and said, "Axel might have done it, and it was my duty. Anyway, we talked, and it turned out that they wanted food and they were willing to trade with us for it."

"How you know, Sidney?" Rotug asked.

"With the language I worked out with you with the bread."

Rotug frowned and said, "That was Axel and bread."

Sidney glanced at Axel, then he shrugged his shoulders and said, "If that's the way you remember it, Rotug. It doesn't matter." He turned back to Axel and went on. "The only things they had to trade were their axes. You remember, Axel, how heavy they are? Our men could hardly lift them much less fight with them." Axel nodded. "I drew pictures in the sand of smaller axes and nodded my head, and I think he understood what I meant.

"He left in the small boat and they all sailed away. That was late in the summer. I expect them to be back in the spring with smaller axes to trade with."

Axel shook his head and said, "That won't help us. Sid needs us now."

Sidney again held his hands up with the palms out and said, "I know. What I was doing was explaining what happened. But, Rotug can go and tell them that if they get Sid back we'll give them all the food they can carry away with them."

"Wonderful," Molly said and looked at Axel.

Axel looked into his wife's eyes for a long moment and shook his head. She frowned as he said, "We can't do that." He was seeing again the burned towns and farms, the graves, the dead stock left in the fields and was thinking of the children who had been taken as slaves. "We can't use a force like that. We wouldn't ever be sure we could control it."

Axel felt a coldness come over him. Was this the right thing to think and do? What about Sid? Was any price too great to pay for his son? For some reason he saw in his mind the balance scale the priest and the blacksmith had used to cheat him. The one with the songbird's egg on one side and the small and very thin coin on the other. He didn't want to be involved in that kind of a deal again, one where someone was going to be hurt.

But then he saw the huge balance scale the butcher had brought the second time he had confronted that same priest, the scale with the large dragon's egg on one side and the bag of gold coins on the other. Maybe there was a way to balance the safety of his son and his desire not to kill again.

If he were to use the blue men and they killed Rohn's knights and destroyed his army, they might keep right on going and burn the town, kill all the people, take the food and children they wanted and sail away. He didn't want to be a part of that happening, but he couldn't just let Sid go either. He had never felt so badly. He wanted someone else to make this decision for him. There wasn't anyone here or anywhere else who could or would do it. He knew he couldn't make the decision now. He had to think about it.

"We can't ask them for help yet. We have to try ourselves first."

Nodding his head, Rotug said, "Rotug go to Rohn castle and capture Sid back."

Molly said, "No. We don't know enough yet." Now Molly counted on her fingers. "We're not even sure he's there. We don't know what the king has planned for Axel. We don't know what Rohn is going to do about the kingdom. We don't know how the rest of the knights feel about Axel being a prince." She opened her palms out and continued, "What we have to do is learn as much as we can before we do anything."

Sid looked at her for a moment, then nodded his head. Axel didn't recognize the way Molly was talking, but then she had never had her baby threatened before. He sure didn't ever want her this mad at him. He said, "Molly's right. We have lots to learn before we can plan anything." He glanced around the dark kitchen making sure they were alone and went on.

"I have to see the king. If he still wants me to be prince and take over when he dies, he'll tell me. . .if he can. Sidney can talk to the knights and see how they feel. Rotug can mix in with the people in town and listen to them talking and maybe he'll come up with something. Good thinking, Molly." He reached over and put his hand on her wrist. "We'll get Sid back."

Molly stood. "What about me? I'm not going to sit in a room somewhere by myself and wait for things to happen. I've got to do something, too." She sat back down and shrugged her shoulders. "The only thing I can think of is going to Rohn's castle and looking for Sid."

Axel shook his head and said, "We can't do that. They might recognize me."

"I wasn't talking about you, Axel. I meant I could go and look for him. You have things to do here while I'm away."

"I couldn't let you go alone, Molly."

Molly looked into Axel's eyes and said with a force Axel wasn't familiar with, "You can't stop me from trying to find my son, Axel."

Axel's voice had a bit of panic in it when he said, "That's not something that women do, Molly. You're not a spy. You don't know what you're doing. They'd catch on and then I'd have to rescue both of you."

11

Sidney stood and paced around the room: to the sink, to the far wall and back to the table. They could hear him talking to himself and see him gesturing with his hands but couldn't understand what he was saying. Shortly he stopped moving and said as he looked at the ceiling, "It could work. . . . It might even work. . .if she'd do it."

Molly reached out her hand and grabbed Sidney's arm and said, "What, Sidney. If I'd do what?"

Axel was shaking his head almost as if he couldn't believe this was his gentle Molly acting this way.

Sidney sat at the table and placed his hands palm down on the surface. He looked at his friends and said, "Molly can do it and it won't be dangerous. She can get into Rohn's castle and look around and talk to people and no one will suspect her of anything."

Axel slammed his palm down and yelled, "No."

Molly put her hand on Axel's, and, looking him in the eyes, said, "Yes, Axel. If I can do it, I have to. Let's listen to Sidney before we decide he's wrong."

Axel sat very still for a moment before he turned to Sidney and smiled as if to say, We'll have to go through the motions here, old friend. What he did say was, "What are you talking about, Sidney?"

"There's a camp of Gypsies near town."

"What is Gypsy?" asked Rotug.

"They travel and put on shows," answered Sidney. "Molly could join them, be part of the band and nobody would suspect her of a thing. They could go to Rohn's castle next and Molly might learn something."

"What could I do as a Gypsy? I can't dance."

"You could sell food."

Axel laughed and said, "What food? Are you suggesting that Molly be a cook for a bunch of travelers?"

"No, she could sell food to the people in the castle. Something that everyone would like."

"Molly make bread good," Rotug said.

Sidney looked at Molly for a moment and said, "Everybody makes bread. You'd have trouble getting people to buy it from a wagon. You'd have to have something to sell that not everybody has or can make."

The group sat at the table and looked at its bleached and scarred surface. Axel sat upright and turned to Molly and said, "You make those thin bread pieces and put honey on them for special times, birthdays and such. I bet people would like them as much as we do, and they sure never would have had it."

Molly nodded and said, "No, not unless they ate in my father's inn. He invented it and sold it as desert."

Sidney said, "You'd have to call it something that people would like to talk about. You could call it bread leaves or something like that."

Axel asked, "How about leaves of bread?"

Sidney shook his head, "Not catchy enough. Won't do. It needs a name that's so strange people will remember it and tell their friends. Like cow's lips."

Molly laughed. "You think people would buy bread with honey on it called cow's lips?"

Sidney looked back down and said, "Maybe not."

Rotug smiled and said, "Why not call bread dragon lips." That be fun to eat."

"That's more fun," Molly said, "They'd remember it but it doesn't sound good. It has to sound good to eat."

Axel clapped his hands. "Dragon ears. We'll call them dragon ears. People'll like the name and they'd be fun to eat. We'll get to talk to everybody in Rohn's castle because they'll all come to the wagon to buy."

Molly frowned at Axel and said, "Not us, Axel, me. Remember they might recognize you? I have to go alone."

"I won't let you do that, Molly. Anything could happen. No, you have to have somebody with you."

"I go with Molly," Rotug said. "We sell dragon ears and talk. I protect Molly. Nobody hurt her or I cut."

Cook flopped down on the far end of the bench by Molly and said, "How do you make dragon ears?"

Molly slid down next to Cook and said, "First, you heat the surface you're going to fry them on and then you take a little flour and a little sour milk and a bit of fat and stir it together until you get a dough." She began using gestures to show what she was saying. "Roll it out on a floured board and then put oil on the hot surface and put the dough on it. Wait a bit and turn it over. Wait again and take it off. After you cut and shape it, make it sweet by dripping a bit of warm honey on it."

The old cook said as she slid closer, "We should practice and see if the men here like them. We could see how much they might be willing to pay and how big they should be and what they should look like." She cackled and continued, "I've never seen a dragon's ear."

Sidney said, "Rotug's seen dragon's ears. He can show you what they look like."

Molly stood and said, "Good. Let's make the dough and Rotug can show us how to shape them."

12

Axel followed Sidney's thin shape out of the kitchen and into the great hall. The two men sat at the long table where the king entertained his guests and where he had been sitting when he had announced that he was adopting Axel, making him the next king.

The table had benches on both sides and was at least 35 feet long, almost half as long as the room was wide. At the end furthest from them was a huge fireplace. It was so wide that a man could stand in the hearth and hold his arms out to the side and not touch the stones of the opening.

There was a fire burning in this one and most of the fireplaces in the castle all winter, for the few windows there were didn't have glass in them. To keep out some of the winter wind, there were heavy curtains that hung clear to the floor. So the fires were needed for heat and light both.

The two leaned toward each other in the cold and dim room and Sidney said, "Tell me about my valley, Axel."

This surprised Axel, because, of course, it wasn't Sidney's valley anymore. He had paid Sidney well for it and it belonged to Axel and Molly now. But, Axel didn't think this was a good time to bring that up.

"First, Sidney, what do you know about what's been going on here that might help me find Sid?" He spread his hands as he said, "Anything at all, Sidney. We're lost about where to begin looking."

"If he's at Rohn's castle, I don't see any way for us to get to him or get him out," Sidney said.

"Us?"

"Us."

"What's that mean? That's not a way for me to find Sid."

Sidney pointed to his chest with twisted fingers and said," I mean *us* to find him. I'm in this, too."

Axel nodded and said, "Sure, sorry, Sidney. You and me. Molly won't be able to do anything, we know that."

"No, we don't."

"We don't what?

"Know that Molly won't be able to find out anything if she goes to Rohn's castle with the Gipsies."

"Sidney, do you really think that plan of her's could work? I wasn't going to let her go. Too dangerous."

"I'm not sure you could stop her and not sure you should if you could."

"I can't lose both of them, Sidney. That would be too much."

"Let's not think that way. Be positive."

Axel nodded and smiled at his old friend. "As always, Sidney, you're right."

Axel shifted his weight on the bench and said, "What have you been doing this last year? Have you been well? Your hands still hurting? Thought up any new firestarters?"

Sidney settled back on the bench and said, "As a mater of fact I have been busy. At first I didn't think there was much to do as the king's wizard. King Willard was too sick to call for me. . .or he didn't care. Either way I never saw him. I was just here."

Sidney spread his hands. Axel thought that he was forcing them to look twisted, but he didn't say anything about it. "He did send one of his men to ask me about a pepper plant that had turned wild and was filling up the fields. It was such a fast grower that it crowded out the other crops. I was supposed to figure out what we could do about it." He stopped talking and looked off across the large room.

"What did you do?"

Sidney brought his eyes back to Axel and said, "I had the village boys collect the peppers from the plants before they could break and spread their seeds. That may stop the plants from spreading. Next spring we'll see if it worked or not."

"What were they like. Hot?"

Sidney hesitated just a bit and said, "I don't think so. The sun was shining but they weren't wearing cloaks."

Axel paused then said, "Sidney. You know I didn't mean the boys. I meant were the peppers hot?"

Sidney laughed and said, "Oh, were the peppers ever hot. They were so hot I had to put them away so they wouldn't dry out and the dust blow around. Just being near a dried pepper was enough to burn your skin into large blisters. Remember how sick the blue men got when the dragon's eggs broke near them?"

"Sure. I'll never forget that."

"Well, this was just as bad or worse. One of the farmer's wives tried to cook one. The fumes burned her skin and they had to move out of the house. Someone tried to go back inside it just last week and they couldn't stand it, it was still so strong."

Axel turned his head to the side and said, "Sidney, they were just peppers, weren't they?"

"I thought so, but I guess not. They started out that way, but the first ones that a farmer planted must have gotten mixed up with a wild pepper or something and produced a new kind."

"So what did you do with all the peppers?"

Sidney nodded when he said, "What I did with the dragon's eggs."

"You dropped them on strangers?"

"No, Axel." Sidney frowned, then continued, "You remember the cave?" Axel nodded, "That's where they are."

"The strangers are in the cave?"

Sidney looked into Axe's eyes for a long moment, then said in a low voice, "You know I meant the peppers, Axel."

"If you can do it, I can, too."

"Go in the cave?"

"Sidney, stop this. We have serious talking to do."

"You're right, Axel. We have to get Sid back, but we can't do anything until we know where he is."

"The only thing that makes any sense to me is that Rohn has him. He's the one who wouldn't want me to come here or to be king when King Willard dies."

"Right, and the only hope we have of knowing where Rohn is keeping him is Molly finding out."

The two men looked at each other and neither spoke. What was there they could say? They didn't know where Sid was. They didn't have any ideas about rescuing him even if they did know. They didn't know what the king would say about it all and even if King Willard still planned on Axel being king.

13

The men left the table and crossed the large room and entered the arched doorway leading to the circular stairs that rose to the floor where King Willard had his chambers. When they reached the top of the stairs and entered the long hallway, they saw a guard at the door to the king's rooms. This man came to attention when he saw them approach and said, "What business do you have here, Sidney, and who is that with you?"

Sidney didn't slow down but stepped around the guard and opened the door. As he did so he said, "Prince Axel. How is he today, guard?"

The guard looked closely at Axel and said, "I haven't heard a thing. The priest was here but that's all I know."

They crossed the large room with the painted ceiling and the rugs hung from the walls that Axel remembered from last year. Where the king used to have his chair, there was a large bed.

King Willard lay covered by blankets, only his face and hands visible. Axel could tell that he'd lost considerable weight, for the covers on the bed were almost flat and he knew that the king had been a very large man, almost fat. He must really be sick, Axel thought.

They stood by the bed for a short time, and the king didn't move or open his eyes. Axel wanted to wake him but didn't know if he should or even if he could.

Axel whispered, "Sidney, he isn't dead is he?"

"I don't know, but I don't think so. Let's leave and come back later. He may be awake then."

When they were in the corridor again, Axel asked, "What have you been working on since I saw you last?"

Sidney stopped walking and said, "What makes you think I've been working on anything, Axel?"

"I know you. You couldn't just sit around. You'd have to be working on something. What is it, a secret?"

"No, of course not. Especially to you. Come on, we'll go down to my workroom and I'll show you."

At the end of one of the darkest passages in the castle, an arched doorway led to stairs that twisted as they followed the curved wall to a lower and even darker level.

Axel followed the black robe and white chicken as Sidney descended and waited as he lit widely spaced torches along the wall. He was talking and his voice echoed from the arched stone ceiling. When he opened a low, wooden door, its hinges creaked, and as they passed through, that sound was followed by a loud screech and the brief but futile beating of wings. Sidney put his free hand to his shoulder and whispered patiently and was answered by a series of soft clucks.

Axel was surprised by what he saw in the room. It looked like no other place he had ever been in. It was very dark and the ceiling was low, though that wasn't too strange. What was different was that the walls all had benches where there were piles of equipment and objects that Axel didn't recognize and couldn't imagine their use.

"What is all this stuff, Sidney?"

"Just what I'm working on."

Axel reached over a small pile of books and picked up a ring the size of a small man's head, but one quarter of the ring was flattened. "What's this for?"

"That's my new stirrup."

Axel turned it over in his hands, shook his head and said, "But it's flat on one side. How's it going to work?"

"It'll work fine, Axel. I even tested it myself. I'm having the blacksmith make some for all the knights."

"But it's flat on one side."

"That's why it's such a good one. You remember how the knights would all limp after they'd been riding all day?"

"Sure."

"Well, why were they limping?"

"I don't know. Their backs hurt for some reason, maybe the wright of all the armor?"

"No, their feet."

"Not their feet, Sidney. They'd been in the saddle, not walking."

"Sit on that bench there and put that stirrup over your foot and pull up on it with both hands and see how that feels."

Axel sat, and holding the ring on the flat side, put it over his right foot and pulled up as hard as he could. "I see what you mean. That hurts where the ring cuts into the sides of my boot."

"Think how much more it would hurt if you had on sixty pounds of armor. Now turn it around and put the flattened side under your arch and pull, and you'll see why the knights like it so much."

Axel did and was surprised at how much better it felt when the weight of his pulling was distributed across the flat side of his foot instead of against the edges. He said, "You been working hard, haven't you, Sidney?"

Sidney crossed the room and put his torch in a holder on the wall and said, "I think this one is going to be good if I ever figure out how a person can move it around."

Axel turned and saw Sidney standing by one of the benches. Fastened to it by clamps was a short but very thick bow about half as long as a man is high. Sidney was pulling back the bowstring with a complicated looking lever on a board which made a cross with the bow. Axel stood next to him and watched as he placed a short arrow in a groove and nocked the end of the shaft in the string, a thick twisting of what looked like horsehide.

"What's that for, Sidney? A child's toy?"

"Just you watch." Sidney crossed the room and opened the thick door. "Here, Axel, could you penetrate this door with that bow you killed the dragons with?"

Axel examined the door. It was two inches thick and made of broad oak planks pegged together. "Of course not. The most an arrow could do is stick in the wood."

Sidney closed and locked the door and returned to the bench and said, "Come back here by this bow." He sighted along the arrow lying in the groove. Axel stood next to him. "I don't know what to call this, but it's going to change the way the king's army fights. This is exciting. This piece here," He indicated a small piece of wood protruding from the bottom of the grooved board, "You pull this piece back and it releases the shaft. Go ahead and shoot the arrow, Axel."

Axel checked along the shaft. He wanted to be sure it would hit the door and not the stones of the wall. He glanced at Sidney and pulled back on the piece of wood Sidney had indicated. The bow jumped, the bench shook and there was a bang against the door. The shaft was gone and the string was humming. Grrr was growling low in his throat and looking at the door. When Axel looked, he expected to see the arrow, but all he could see were about two inches of the shaft with the fletching on it.

"Go look at the door, Axel," Sidney said as he handed him the key.

When he had unlocked and opened the door, Axel was amazed to see the front of the shaft sticking out of the outside of the door. It had pierced the two inches of dried oak. "Sidney, this is a wonderful invention, but if the shaft will go through this door, it'll sure go through a knight's armor."

Sidney nodded proudly and said, "Right."

"This is too dangerous to use, Sidney. If the wrong people got hold of this, they could kill any armored man they wanted to. You have to destroy it before anyone sees it."

"But then the king wouldn't have it either."

"It's better that way. This could change war as we know it. No army could stand against something as powerful as this. I'll help you take it apart and we'll never tell anyone about it," Axel started to loosen the clamps.

Sidney put his hand on Axel's shoulder and said, "We can't do that, Axel. If the king doesn't have it, someone else might come up with it. . .if they have a truly smart wizard that is. What if Rohn's archers had some of these?"

"He will as soon as he sees this thing work. He'll figure out how to make them and then both sides will have them."

"That might be good. If both sides had bows that could shoot through armor, then the knights wouldn't be so eager to fight. This might be the end of war, Axel. You've always talked like you thought that would be a good idea."

Axel saw in his mind the king's knights lined up on their horses facing the archers of some army. The horses charged, the archers fired, the short shafts sank into the knights' chests and stuck out of the armor covering their backs. The armored men collapsed and fell from their mounts. "No, Sidney, this is too powerful. You have to promise me you'll destroy this machine."

"I'll think about it, Axel, but I can't promise anything." He turned and pointed to a bench, "Look over here." He crossed the small room and stood by the bench. Against one wall were a number of wooden pails and bulging, small, but heavily loaded sacks. He stooped, examining the contents of the pails, until he found one that satisfied him.

Taking it and two of the sacks, he motioned for Axel to follow and retraced their path up the stairs, shutting the door at the top. With Cynthia bobbing on his shoulder and Axel and Grrr following closely behind, he climbed a new stairway to a heavy door, felt in a pocket of his cloak and brought out a another key which he used to unlock it.

After putting the bucket and sacks by a bench against the far wall, he returned to the door and carefully looked both ways down the dim corridor, then he shut his eyes and, tilting his head, listened for a moment before softly closing the door.

After taking measured portions of materials from the bucket and each of the bags and placing them in a crude stone bowl, he stirred the mixture slowly with a wooden spoon and poured into it a bit of liquid from a glass flask that he'd taken from a shelf above the bench. This he again stirred while carrying the bowl to the one small window, the only source of light in the dark room.

When he was satisfied with the mixture, he returned to the bench and gently set the bowl down and pulled from a small cloth bag a thin stick about as long as one of his fingers. He dipped this into the bowl and, after turning it, lifted it out. The end was coated with a dark bulb of the mixture.

He set the dry end of the stick into a hole drilled in a short board. It looked like the firestarter he had given Axel. He set this on the edge of the bench. Turning pages as he walked, he read from a leather-covered book, the pages brittle and cracking in his fingers. His voice was soft and uninflected, and when he finished reading, he shut the book and said, "I've been working on the idea of the firestarter and came up with something I've got to ask you about. The mixture I've got now is pretty powerful, Axel, so you better not stand so near. Stand over by the door."

He selected a piece of flint from the bench and struck it against a bit of metal fastened to the board near the stick. Sparks danced as he repeatedly struck the flint.

A brilliant flash of light lit the dim room, which was quickly filled from the shelf up by clouds of smoke. Cynthia screamed; Sidney yelled and danced as he slapped at his clothing. He stumbled into the corridor in clouds of dark smoke, his chicken clutching tightly to the cloth on his shoulder, but she was looking around frantically, her eyes wide. She scolded Sidney loudly and flapped her blackened and almost featherless wings.

Sidney looked for Axel and, when he didn't see him in the smoky hall, reentered the room. Axel was still by the far bench but now covered in soot and was rubbing his eyes and coughing.

When he could tell that Axel wasn't hurt, he held Cynthia in front of his face and examined the dark stubs of her feathers. "I've been wanting to cook and eat this bird for some time now. You hungry, Axel?"

Axel was coughing and spitting up black soot. He was shocked both by the blast and Sidney's attitude toward his pet. "You can't eat that chicken; she's your pet, Sidney."

"Just kidding, my boy," He lifted the burnt bird and examined her closely, "She's already half cooked."

"The fire must have jumped to the bowl," Sidney said as he walked to the bench. "Sure it did. Look here, Axel. The bowl's empty, burnt and split. It all burned up at the same time. That's why there was such an big flash." He laughed, "It works good doesn't it?"

Axel was looking at Cynthia. "On chickens it does."

14

Molly sprinkled oil on the hot surface and turned the dough over. The sheet of iron that covered the stove smoked when the oil hit it and added to the clouds that were already filling the kitchen. But there was a satisfying sizzle and she smiled at Cook, who was interested in how Molly was making this new kind of bread but was in doubt about whether it would be any good.

When the flat piece was done, it was golden brown and had a rough bubbled texture. Molly picked it off the stove with a wooden spatula and set it on the table. "While it's still hot we have to cut and shape it," she said, and she quickly ran a knife over the surface of the thin bread, cutting it into triangles the size of a man's hand.

She looked at the table where Rotug had been sitting and he was gone.

Moving quickly, she curled each piece slightly so that it resembled a large pointed ear. Her dragon's ears.

When they had finished dripping honey on the inside of the ears, they had three baskets filled and were ready to find out how the king's knights liked them.

15

Sid stood on the short bench and leaned back and could see a bit of sky through a small window in the wall. It's blue so it must be nice out, he thought. Being in here wasn't as bad as it could be; at least he had bread to eat and there was a bucket of water he could drink, but he was chained to the wall by his left ankle and that was very uncomfortable.

It was dark in the room and the chain was heavy enough that when he moved he fell and scraped his knees on the stone floor. He was alone, chained, and in silence.

He hadn't been awake long before he heard a loud voice in the hallway. A softer voice responded and Sid could tell that the loud voice was giving commands and the softer one was answering.

Soon men stopped by his door and when he heard a key turning the lock, he sat on the bench next to the small table and watched his door. The men entering carried a lantern so that when the door opened, the room was flooded with yellow light that seemed very bright to Sid. He held his hand up to shield his eyes and listened to the footsteps as they approached.

When the men were close to him, Sid looked up. There were two. The one with the loud voice was dressed in black and had a full black beard, much like Rotug's, but, of course, much darker. The other man was the guard who had brought him here last night.

The large man stood over Sid, and, without saying anything, cuffed him on the side of the head. It hurt. Sid had never been hit before and this was a shock. That big man had hit him, maybe not as hard as he could have, but hard enough to knock him off the bench and onto the floor. He scrambled away from the men on his hands and knees, as far as the chain would allow. When it stopped him, he stood and said, "My father will know that you hit me." He was surprised at how small his voice sounded.

"Sit on the bench, boy," the bearded man commanded.

Sid put his hand over his ear which was still ringing, and, rubbing it, said, "You can't make me do what you want. Nobody can but my parents."

The large man grabbed the chain where it was fastened to the wall and gave it a jerk. Sid's leg was pulled violently to the side and he stumbled toward the bench. When Sid was close enough to him, the man grabbed a handful of Sid's hair and pulled him to the bench and forced him to sit.

"Yeow." Sid couldn't stop himself from yelling out.

When he was seated, the man knelt on one knee in front of him and said, "This doesn't have to hurt, boy. All I want to know is what your father's planning to do. If you tell me we'll turn you loose, and someone will take you home. If you don't tell me what I want to know, well. . .we'll see."

Sid decided right then that no matter what was done to him he wasn't going to say anything about his father.

"I don't care what you do. I'm not going to tell you."

The man stood and smiled down at Sid and said, "You just got here. You got fire in you yet. We'll give you a couple of days and see what you have to tell me."

The large man turned, and, without saying anything more, left the room. The one with the lantern followed and locked the door, and Sid could hear their footsteps as they walked away.

For the first time in his young life, Sid was really scared. He'd never been all alone before. His parents had always been within calling distance, but here, no matter how loud he yelled, he knew no one would hear him or care. He felt very cut off from everyone. There wasn't anybody to talk to and he missed his parents a lot and Grrr and even Rotug.

A guard brought him food two times a day and a pail of water and emptied his slops bucket. On the third day they took off his ankle chain. That was better.

He had no doubt his father would find him, for wasn't his father a knight and even a prince? He could do this if he could kill dragons and save the whole kingdom from barbarians.

That made Sid think about Rotug as a barbarian. It was hard to see the gentle giant as a killer cutting knights in half with that monster of an axe. He'd found Rotug's axe one day in the barn when he'd taken Rotug some food and he wasn't in his room. The axe had been leaning against the wall and Sid just had to pick it up and swing it. He tried and wasn't able to lift it off the floor. It would take a really strong person to use that. He was doubly proud of his father and Sidney for driving the barbarians into the sea.

When Sid wasn't thinking about home he listened for the sounds that would tell him that there were other prisoners in other cells. He concentrated on the silence so hard that he began to hear voices he knew were in his head. He didn't think there were any other prisoners nearby. There were no sounds at all. He was alone and no one knew where he was.

16

Axel wiped the soot from his face and said, "That mixture might be extreme just to light a fire, Sidney."

"No, no, Axel. It wasn't supposed to make a big fire like that. But it was something wasn't it? We'll have to try that again. . . . Maybe we should be outside?"

"Why do it again? You know what it does now. Isn't that good enough?"

"I could learn something, maybe."

"What?"

"I don't know. If I knew what I'd learn there'd be no point in doing it again."

"What do you want to learn?"

"I don't know that either."

Axel pounded at his clothes and waved away the dust and soot that surrounded him. "When you do it again, let me know and I'll make sure I'm busy somewhere else."

"We have to work together, Axel. We might learn something that'll help us get Sid back. You never know."

"If I thought so I'd do anything, you know that."

As the two walked down the stairs, Sidney said, "That was an interesting event there. If we think about it we might come up with something."

"Sure we could. If I'd had some of that stuff I could have killed a dragon real easy."

Sidney stopped walking and asked, "How?"

"Axel shrugged his shoulders and thought for a moment and said, "I could have shot some of it on arrows into them. . . . Same thing isn't it?"

"Sure it is, Axel. What we did that was different this time was that we blew up a whole bowl of the mixture. That's where the smoke and fire came from. If the bowl hadn't been there, the firestick would have caught on fire. I've been looking for a better mixture to make it easier to light the firestick. What we have to think about is what happened when the bowl blew up."

"Why?"

"Because we have to know things."

"Sure, Sidney, go ahead and think about it."

They sat at the long table in the great room, one on each side, and Sidney said, "If we're going to use this new finding to help us, we have to study it."

"How do we do that?"

"We talk about it."

Axel shook his head impatiently, "Sidney, we were both there. We both know what happened. What good will it be to tell each other what happened? We already know."

"It's the analysis that's important, Axel." Sidney held out his hands and looked Axel in the eyes and said, "Come on and help me. I need your thinking."

Axel looked at his friend with a serious expression and said, "Sure, Sidney, I'm thinking about what happened."

"What have you got?"

"What?"

"What do you think?"

"Why don't you help me think about finding Sid, Sidney? You used to help me think and we always came up with some good ideas."

"We'll have to look at getting Sid back as a problem."

"It is a problem," Axel said louder than he meant to, and he clenched his hands together on the table's top.

"We have to look at what we have, then at how that might help us."

"Right."

"I'll make a list. We have Rotug, Molly, the fire-starter's new mixture that burns fast, the stick bow that shoots so good. . .and that's it."

"We have more than that," Axel said. "We have all those peppers you have in the cave."

"What good are they?"

"That comes later. Now all we're doing is listing what we have, isn't it?"

"Sorry."

"We have Molly's dragon ears, Rotug's axe—"

"You let that barbarian bring his huge axe?"

"How would you have stopped him?"

Sidney thought for a moment, then he said with a smile, "Sure, I see what you mean. But, we have something that we haven't listed yet. You're the prince and are going to be king. That ought to be good for something."

The two men sat and looked into each other's eyes for a long time, both men thinking of their problem and having no ideas about how to solve it. Finally Axel asked, "How many peppers are there in the cave, Sidney?"

Sidney petted Cynthia briefly, wiped the feather soot off his hand onto his cloak, and, lifting his other hand, said, "You remember how big a pile of eggs there was?"

"There can't be that many peppers in the whole kingdom, Sidney."

"I know that. I was just trying to find a way to describe how many there are. Visualize that wall of dragon eggs in your mind and then make a small pile next to it. About one pepper for each egg. About that many."

"Are they dried out or are they still whole?"

"They were whole when I stored them. They'd be dried out by now. I sure don't want to go down there to find out. They could have broken. That's one thing we have to know about before we decide what to do. We've got to examine those peppers."

"What for?"

"We could learn something, maybe."

"What?"

"Axel, I don't know. If I knew what we'd learn there wouldn't be a point in doing it cause we'd already know."

"What do you think you might learn?"

Sidney shook his head. "I don't know that either."

"This sounds familiar to me."

"It should."

"Now, let's talk about that new firestarter stuff."

"You may have noticed I don't have it perfected yet. All it did was burn fast. Like the dragons did when you shot arrows into their mouths. You said the dragons blew up, but what happened was that the gas in their stomachs burned so fast that there was no place for it to go since it was trapped in the dragon's stomach. That must have caused lots of pressure. And ka-boom"

"Ka-boom?"

"Sure, the sound of a dragon blowing up. Wait," Sidney held up one finger then rubbed the top of his head with his palm. He jumped from the bench and began to walk along his side of the table, his hands gesturing and his voice just loud enough for Axel to tell that he was talking but not loud enough for Axel to understand what he was saying. But he could hear an occasional word, "Cave. . .dragon. . .large stone. . .smoke. . .splash."

"What is it Sidney? You having an idea?"

"I don't know yet Axel. You have to tell me about the dragons blowing up. Give me as much detail as you can remember. Tell me everything."

17

A sound from the hallway told Sid that someone was outside his cell. The steps weren't even; one foot dragged on the stone floor. There was the thud of one boot and the slow sliding of the other. . .then the thud again. The sounds stopped at his door. A rustle of clothing and a jangling of metal against metal and Sid could hear the key turn in the old lock.

As the door swung inward, Sid shielded his eyes from the light the man had brought with him. It had been totally black in his cell until then, but the slight draft of the opening door made the flame waver and cast wild shadows along the walls made of large stones, and in some places there were dark streaks where water had run down the blocks. The floor, too, was made of slabs of stone and there was a pile of straw in one corner.

Sid stood and faced the man. He was scared, but his father had told him that the thing to do when he was scared was to face the fear. It never helped to turn away or to hide; it only made it worse. Sid decided that he couldn't show even the least fear, so he said in as loud a voice as he could, "You must let me go. My father, the prince, will be very upset with you if you keep me here just one hour longer." He was surprised that his "loud" voice sounded so small and thin.

The man put the lantern on the small table and his voice grated as he spoke. It sounded to Sid like when Rotug had used his father's file to sharpen his axe.

"Come here, boy. Sit at the table."

Sid wasn't going to cooperate in any way with this man. "I'm going to stand right here until you let me go."

The man's hand moved so fast that Sid didn't see it in the dim light. He knew that the man had moved when he was jerked by the arm toward the bench. The hand pulled down and Sid realized he was sitting.

"You can't do this to me," Sid yelled. He spun on the bench and, bringing his leg back, shot out his foot and caught the man between the legs with it. Sid had kicked out as hard as he could, and when the man bent over and moaned, Sid ran out the door. He had no idea which way to go in the dark hallway, but the guards had always come from the right, so he turned that way and ran into the darkness. He could hear the man trip over the bench and even the thud as his body hit the stone floor.

The hallway ended with a wall of stone, but there were stairs leading up on the right. There was light at the top and Sid thought that there could be men there. He sure didn't want to run into anyone else, so he turned to his left and there was a depression in the wall. With effort, he could just force himself into it but knew that it wasn't a good place to hide. He'd have to move, maybe go the opposite way down past his cell. A thud and scrape told him that the guard was coming, but it was getting no lighter. In his hurry to follow Sid, the man must have left the lantern. Sid closed his eyes. If he couldn't see the guard, maybe in the darkness the guard wouldn't see him.

And the guard didn't. He turned up the stairs and disappeared beyond the light. There was a clang of metal hitting something hard and the cellar was silent again. Sid pushed his way out of his hiding place and ran back past his cell. Here the hallway was very dark, so he returned to the cell for the lantern.

18

Axel said, "Sidney, I told you about them blowing up when I first returned to the valley. You know everything I know about what happened to them. And, we don't have dragon trouble, so what good would that do?"

Sidney sounded impatient now, "Just do it, Axel. Start with the first one and tell me everything. It may help and if I'm right, it will."

"You figured out something." Axel grabbed Sidney by the arm and squeezed. "Tell me."

Sidney pulled his arm away and said, "I don't know anything yet, because you haven't told me about the explosions."

Leaning forward on his elbows brought his nose close to the material of his cloak, and Axel could smell the burned wool. He leaned back and started with the first dragon. There wasn't much he could tell Sidney about the dragon blowing up because he'd been knocked out by the blast. He did describe the pieces of dragon he'd found all over the shelf in front of the cave and how some of the beast had been blown over the edge and down by Winthton. When he started to tell Sidney about the second dragon, the one at Tightly in the cave by the sea, Sidney stopped him.

"Stop, Axel. This is the part I want you to think very carefully about. I have to know it all. So, start with when you first got to the cave and I have to know what you saw, what you felt, what you smelled, and most of all, what you think happened."

Axel shifted his body on the bench so that he was facing the arch that led to the courtyard, shook his head and said, "What's this all for, Sidney?"

"I'll tell you if I think of something. Now do as I ask, for Sid's sake."

Axel nodded and talked slowly so as to remember as much as he could of that cold morning on the shelf by the water. "I remember I was stiff from the cold and the waiting. I'd been kneeling behind the boulder for almost an hour and it was getting hard—"

Sidney put both his palms out toward Axel and said, "Stop right there, Axel. This is what I meant, I need to know everything, and I don't know anything about this boulder. Now I want details."

Axel felt like he had failed and resolved to give Sidney exactly what he wanted. "Just inside the arch that rose over the entrance to the dragon's cave, there was a big boulder, as large I am. When I got behind it and leaned against it, it moved. It seemed to me to be too big to move so easy, so I pushed against it and it was really light. It was still too dark to see good, but I felt over my side of it and I could feel holes and dents all over it's surface. I waited behind it for first light. Is that what you want?"

Pointing his finger at Axel, Sidney said, "Good. Exactly what I wanted you to do. Now, talk about what it felt like and how it moved again."

Shaking his head, Axel said, "That was well over a year ago. I'm not sure I remember it all that clearly."

Sidney smiled and said, "Sure you can, Axel. Just try."

With his eyes tightly shut, Axel thought back to that damp morning he had spent on the ledge over the water. He could remember again how the water smelled of cold seaweed and how his back and knees hurt from kneeling behind the big stone. When he turned, in his mind, and looked at the water, he saw again the thin pink line that meant that the sun was about to come up and the dragon would be coming out of the cave.

"I remember that I was surprised that the stone was so light. Like it was hollow or something. I know that because it moved when I leaned against it."

"Talk about that."

"I leaned with my. . .right hand. I held it in front of me and put it on the boulder and leaned out to look for the dragon. That's when it rocked a bit.

"I remember that the dragon had made a small noise. I saw a slight shifting of the dark shadows deep in the back of the cave. I strained my eyes to make out shapes. Then the morning sunlight reflected off its scales, and I knew I was looking at the dragon. I couldn't see it well yet, but it was moving slowly. I remember thinking that it was cold from the night. Its skin was a shiny green and black and looked damp, like leather clothing worn in the rain. I remember thinking, It's coming to the mouth of the cave to warm itself in the sun.

"I moved back behind the boulder. I remember that I didn't like not being able to see where the dragon was, but I couldn't let it see me before I was ready for it.

"I heard its claws scrape and cut the stone floor, and when it reached the large part of the entrance, just where the sides of the cave began to open up, it opened its wings a little—"

"There, that part. Talk about that."

Axel smiled at his friend as if to say, This is silly. But he went on. "I could hear the leather slap as the dragon shook the dampness out of its wings—"

"No, the part about where you said something about the cave opening up."

"The opening was wide enough, but the further back it got the smaller it got. I remember thinking it was like a funnel."

"Good, go on."

"The dragon hadn't seen or smelled me yet, and I knew I'd have to stay behind the boulder until it got close enough that I could get a clear shot. I could hear it breathe now. Long rasping breaths, like it was dying or in pain or something.

"I wasn't sure when it was close enough. I didn't dare lean out to look to make sure. But, it must have stopped moving toward me, because there wasn't any more noise from it. I was afraid to make my move for fear it was too soon and afraid not to make my move before it was too late. I leaned around the stone to look, and the dragon was still deep enough in the cave that its upper half was in darkness, and I couldn't see its head well enough to put an arrow in its mouth. I was scared. I knew I couldn't make a mistake. I wouldn't get two shots."

Sidney was grinning when he said, "This is just what I wanted, keep going," and he nodded to encourage Axel.

"As soon as I saw its opened mouth, I fired and jumped behind the boulder, but I tripped on something and I remember I fell against it. When I did, it began to roll down the incline toward the inside of the cave and the dragon. When the boulder rolled into the cave, it almost filled the mouth and continued down into the darkness. It must have pushed the dragon back in front of it. I jumped to one side of the opening and stood with my back against the wall of the cliff and waited for the explosion.

"And that's all I remember. What's this good for, Sidney? We've got some serious planning to do and we're sitting here talking about killing dragons."

Sidney nodded and said, "Just a bit more. Go on."

Axel sighed and continued. "The boulder flew out of the mouth of the cave. I remember it went real high. I turned and watched it against the lighter sky as it sailed out over the waves. It landed with a big splash. Flame and red and black smoke rolled out of the opening just next to where I was standing. I could feel the blast against my back as the rock face of the cliff shook.

"While the smoke was being blown away by the wind, I tried to clear my ears by pounding on the sides of my head. They felt plugged up, and there was a ringing sound that was painful. When I looked out over the water, I could see that the surface still had rings in it from where the boulder landed."

Sidney jumped up and started pacing back and forth in front of his friend. "This really helps, Axel. I think I know what we can do. But we have to hurry. There're lots of parts to this plan and they all have to be right if it's going to work."

"What plan?"

"My plan. Come with me, Axel," Sidney hurried from the room toward the courtyard.

19

Rotug was not a patient man. In his kingdom, if someone did something against you, you cut him in half.
People there didn't sit around and discuss ways to sneak
and trick people. A man had a job to do, he did it, and
then they'd sit around the fire and talk about it later.

This was enough discussing the problem. He had to get
Sid back. Sid was little and scared. He was a good boy
and worth saving. Rotug walked to the stable and asked a
man there where their horses were. When he found
Winthton, he asked another worker where their packs
were.

Rotug opened the bundle with their things in it and
unstrapped his axe. He wrapped it in a blanket to hide
what it was and headed for the entrance to the castle. The
first man he talked to saw the giant and his huge package
and it reminded him of the blue men who had invaded his
country a year ago. "Hey, you. Stop."

Rotug either didn't hear him or he pretended not to. In
either case, he ignored the man and walked out of the
courtyard and over the moat and turned at the road that
went past the castle. He was headed toward the beach.
There had to be a boat there. He was headed home. He
would get some of his countrymen and come back and
they would cut the knights of Rohn. If they had to, they
would cut the whole army. They would find Sid and take
him back. He would save the son of his friend. Axel had
saved him when he needed help. Now he would pay him
back. Rotug did not owe anybody anything. He paid his
debts.

A cold and sharp wind, pushing both waves and light
gray clouds in front of it, tossed salty spray and fish smell

over the small inlet near the castle. A short, white and blue boat was pulled up on the shale beach, its sail furled. A fisherman, his face dark and lined above his beard, his hands hard and scarred from pulling on rough rope in cold waters, was mending his net by the boat. He was sitting on the rough beach stones with the net piled beside him and in his lap.

Working with a notched piece of wood and a bole of twine, he worked at the net and but watched Rotug when he stopped and looked over the boat. His voice was rough and full of phlegm. "What do you need, Stranger?"

"I look at boat."

The man laughed and said, "I can see that. That's why I asked."

"Why you ask?"

"It's my boat."

"Is good boat?"

"Sure it is. Why are you asking about it?"

"I need boat."

The fisherman didn't like the way this conversation was going. This strange man was the largest person he had ever seen and he talked different. He stood and found that he came only to the man's chest. He looked up at Rotug and said, "It's my boat and I need it."

Rotug said, "You sail boat for Rotug," and he put his great hand on the man's shoulder. The man staggered, but saved himself from a fall by holding onto the side of his boat.

"Now, Stranger, I don't know who you think you are, but—"

"I am Rotug. I need boat. You sail boat for me now. I pay later." He smiled at the small fisherman. "If you want Rotug to pay."

74

The fisherman was rubbing his shoulder where Rotug had held it and was looking around for help when Rotug reached out to place his hand on the other shoulder. When he saw the gesture, the fisherman jumped back and said, "Sure Stranger, where you want to go?"

"I tell when in boat." Rotug put the wrapped axe in the boat and with ease picked up the bow and slid the boat into the water. The fisherman balled up his net, and, throwing it into the boat as it went by, followed Rotug into waist deep water.

"Get in boat," Rotug said as he held one end up so the other end rode low and the man could climb in. When he was seated, Rotug pushed his end of the boat down till the water was almost over the sides and jumped in and sat and said, "You make sail move boat. I say where we go."

20

Sidney led Axel to the pottery shed where a woman was working on a wheel making clay pots. The woman had a long thin face above a very slender body. Her hands were so covered in gray clay that it looked as if her fingers were webbed.

It was a low shed and very hot, for in the back there was a mound of flat stones covering a very hot pit of burning charcoal. She had put three pots on a grate under the covering of stones and was telling a young boy who was pumping a bellows that the fire had to be much hotter.

When she turned back to her wheel, she saw the two men looking at her. Using her forearm, she pushed strands of her long, brown hair away from her face and smiled at the two men. Sidney said, "We need a special pot made for the king."

She knew who Sidney was and knew that he was the king's wizard. She nodded her head and looked down. "Show me some small pots about this big," Sidney held his hands in the shape of a small gourd. "About the size of a man's fist."

When the woman stood, Axel noticed that she was younger than he thought, but she was very dirty. Not just with the dried clay on her arms and face, but the charcoal dust that hung in the air filled the creases in her skin and the slight lines in her face. She went to a shelf in the side of the stall and handed Sidney a pot.

Sidney turned it in his hands and said, "This is the right size, but can you make me lots of them that don't have handles? They have to be perfectly round with no lips." He pointed out what he meant. There has to be a small hole that can be plugged up with rags."

She looked at the pot for a moment then at Sidney and asked, "How many do you need?"

"About twenty would do fine to practice with."

"What is twenty?"

Sidney held up both hands with the fingers spread, then he reached over and held up Axel's hands and spread his fingers and then his own again and smiled at the woman. She looked from one of them to the other and laughed. "I'll make the king twenty pots just like you ask for."

"When?"

"The woman smiled at Sidney and asked, "When are you coming back?"

"Three days."

"Not for three days?" The woman brushed the hair away from her face again and looked at him out of the sides of her eyes.

Axel was surprised to see that Sidney's face was flushed. Maybe it was the heat in the shed, he thought.

Sidney picked up the pot they had been looking at and said, "I'll take this one with me now." He smiled at the potter-woman and turning, walked into the gray light of the courtyard. Axel couldn't make any sense of what was happening, but he followed his friend across the courtyard to the blacksmith's shop.

The large blacksmith was making arrowheads. He had been doing that all day, every day for a month. The king had ordered that there be a big buildup of arms. The blacksmith was a powerful man, but strangely stooped. Maybe it was from bending over his work all day. His arms were massive, at least the one Axel could see was.

But when he turned, Axel could see that the man's left arm was only about half the size. Strange, he thought.

The blacksmith looked up and saw two men standing in the doorway to his shop. He recognized Sidney right away, but even though the other man looked familiar, he didn't recognize him until they came into the shop and stood close.

"Is that Sir Axel?" he asked, looking up from his bent-over position and reached out and grasped Axel's hand and shook it. Axel had never felt a hand so hard. It was not only strong, but it felt as rough to his palm as a stone wall.

"It's good to see you again, Blacksmith. It's been over a year since we last talked. How have you been?"

The large man turned to Sidney and said, "I made Sir Axel the stars and hooks he used to kill the dragons with." Axel couldn't see his lips move because of his very heavy beard but the voice was loud. "He's a real hero in this kingdom."

Sidney nodded and said, "I know you do good work. The king needs an unusual weapon made. He wants you to make him a metal cave."

"A what?"

Sidney stepped closer and said in a lower voice. "It's not really a cave," He glanced at Axel as if for help, then went on, "but it has to be made like one."

"Sir Axel can tell ya that I can make anything ya can draw. Isn't that right, Sir Axel?" He turned toward Axel and raised his large, dark eyebrows.

Axel grinned and said, "This man can make anything you want, Sidney, but it'd help if you could draw him a picture of it."

"I can't draw. Never could."

Axel picked up a piece of charcoal from the floor and said, "You describe what you need and I'll draw it on the wall here." When he stepped to the wall he could see the faint lines he had drawn when he had asked the blacksmith to make the three-pronged hooks with the wedges connected to them by chains.

Sidney came and stood next to Axel and said, "You told me that the boulder rolled into the cave, and when the dragon blew up, it shot out of the mouth of the cave, right?" Axel nodded. "What we need is a metal cave and we can shoot it at Rohn's men."

"Shoot a cave at Rohn's men?"

Sidney was impatient, "Not shoot the cave."

Axel looked at Sidney for as long as he could stand it, then said, "You're talking about shooting dragons out of a metal cave?"

"No. We shoot the pots out of the cave."

Axel turned and walked out of the blacksmith's shop, tossing the piece of charcoal into the forge. Sidney said, "Wait, Axel. I need you here. Come and draw on the wall when I describe what we'll need."

Axel turned, and talking to the darkness, said, "Tell me first. If I understand what you're talking about, I'll draw it for you, but I don't think this is what we need to be doing to get Sid back." He walked back into the shop and selected another piece of charcoal and again stood facing the wall and looked at his friend.

Sidney stood next to him and said slowly, "Draw the cave where the stone shot out, but draw it sideways."

"I don't understand how to do that. What does a sideways cave look like?"

"It's not sideways, it's just the drawing that's sideways. You said it was wider at the mouth than it was further back in, didn't you?" Axel nodded. "Then draw the opening of the cave on the wall."

Axel started with the shelf where he'd been standing, and Sidney stopped him. "Just the mouth of the cave." Axel drew an uneven circle. "Good. Now pretend that we can see the rest of the cave from the side, right through the rock." Axel frowned and bit his lip. "The front of the cave should be as big as the opening, right?" Axel nodded again. "Then it should start to get narrower the further back it goes."

Axel said, "Oh, I know what you mean," and he started drawing. "Like this?" He had a gradually narrowing tunnel back from the opening.

Sidney stood back and studied the drawing. He was nodding his head. He smiled and said, "Now draw the boulder."

Axel drew the boulder to be about half as big as the cave entrance. It was the way he remembered it. When he was done he turned and looked at Sidney.

"Now draw the whole thing again, only make it look like something the blacksmith can make us."

"He can't make us a mountain with a cave in it, Sidney."

"All we need is the cave. If he makes the cave and leaves out the mountain, we'll have a metal cave. We should be able to pick it up and carry it around with us."

"Sidney, the opening of that cave was taller than I am."

"And that was important because the boulder was big. But, if we want to shoot small things like this pot here, it can be small." He pointed to the wall and said, "Draw a metal cave that this would fit into."

Axel started drawing and muttered under his breath as he did so.

"What's the matter, Axel?"

"There," Axel said, stepping back. "But, you'll never find baby dragons small enough to stuff in anything that size."

Sidney was studying the drawing. "What's this about baby dragons?"

As if he were talking to a child who wasn't very bright, Axel explained. "The boulder was between the dragon and the opening of the cave. I shot the arrow just after I had leaned against the boulder. It started rolling and I shot the arrow. I couldn't see the dragon when it blew up. It was behind the boulder. It must have been trapped back in there."

Sidney jumped up and down and yelled, "Now you got it, Axel. I knew you'd understand what I wanted. We'll have an exploding cave that can push out pots and send them a long way. We just need one more thing and we'll have it."

Axel was losing patience. He said, "What will we have, Sidney?"

"I don't know what to call it, Axel, but it'll be a combination of an exploding dragon and a cave." Sidney was getting excited now. "We could call it a name that's a part of both of those things."

The blacksmith was catching some of the excitement. "What things?"

"A dragon and a cave. We could call it a dragcave."

Axel said, "That would be hard to say. Can't we think of a combination of words that would sound better?"

"How about cavedrag? Sidney said."

Axel shook his head.

"Congave?"

Axel said the word a number of times to himself. Shook his head and said, "That's way too mixed up to work with."

Sidney threw up his hands and yelled, "Oh, all right, we'll call it a cavgon then."

Axel smiled and said, "That's a lot better, but it's not right yet. We may have to think about it some more while we search for some tiny dragons."

Sidney shook his head and said to the blacksmith. "The cavgon you make has to be strong so that it doesn't blow apart like the dragons did. It has to be closed at one end so the pots can only go out the other end."

Axel was getting into it now. "We'll need very tiny little arrows to shoot into the mouth of the cavgon at the baby dragons."

Sidney turned and was about to say something about how dumb that was when he stopped and looked hard at Axel, and said, "You know, that's right. We have to have a way to get fire into the back of the cavgon after the pot's put in the end." He turned and looked at the drawing.

"Blacksmith, you can help here. Look at this drawing and tell us how we can get fire to this place here." Sidney drew a circle half way down the cave and pointed to the closed end.

The blacksmith studied the drawing for some time and finally said, "Make a hole and put fire in that way."

Sidney studied the drawing and said, "Show me."

Using another piece of charcoal, the blacksmith drew a small circle in the end of the cave. He turned and smiled at Sidney. "Like so."

"Could you make the king something like this, Blacksmith?"

"Sure. I can make anything that anybody can draw."

Axel said, "Can you find us some tiny dragons if we draw a picture of one for you?"

The blacksmith frowned, but before he could say anything, Sidney said, "Do it, Blacksmith. And make the cavgon just big enough that this pot will fit snug in the middle of it. But it has to be strong enough that. . ." He shrugged his shoulders and as he handed the pot to the blacksmith, turned toward Axel and smiled. "An exploding tiny dragon won't break it." He turned and started to move toward the doorway and said, "We've still got lots to do, Axel. Let's go."

21

Sid ran as fast as he could carrying the lantern. He could hear commotion at the far end of the corridor just before he turned a corner. Here the hall split. One way was no better than the other, so he turned left and ran with the light creating a large Sid on the wall next to him.

Set into the wall was an iron ladder. He knew he'd be trapped in the tunnel if he didn't find a way out. If he climbed the ladder, the man coming would see the light. He blew it out and started climbing. He had to take the lantern with him, for if he left it on the floor at the foot of the ladder, the men would know where he was.

It was hard climbing with just one hand, but he had no choice. That or be caught. The ladder led to a short shelf. Sid clambered onto it. The footsteps were closer now and he could hear the men talking to each other. He wiggled back as far as he could and lay still.

When the men turned the corner their voices became much louder and the light they carried made the ceiling brighter. They hurried past below him and the sounds they made became muted and the light dimmed.

Sid felt along the walls for a way out. His hands struck a metal grating. It was solid, and Sid knew he'd never get out that way. Now he knew why the men hadn't considered that he could get away up the ladder. He had no choice but to take the stairs at the other end of the hallway. Leaving the lantern, he hurried down the ladder.

Which way to go? He had to visualize which side of the hall the ladder had been on when he first came to it. It had been on his left. That meant that he'd have to turn to the right when he got to the floor. Or was it to the left? He'd be facing the ladder, so should he turn around

facing the hall? No time to think longer on it. He scuffled
his feet straight ahead until he touched the opposite wall,
then turned to the right and ran with his hand touching the
stone blocks. It wouldn't do to come to a corner and
knock himself out by running into the wall.

Sid changed sides of the hall. His right hand was
touching the wall. He remembered that the stairs were on
the right and when he couldn't feel the wall anymore,
he'd know that he was at the end of the hall.

At the top of the stairs there was a large wooden door,
but the men had left it open. Through the door there was
some light. There were torches widely spaced along the
wall. More stairs, on the left this time. Up and another
hallway. And daylight. A small door with a barred
window was standing ajar.

On the other side of the door was the courtyard he had
seen when he had first been brought to the castle. Sid
looked carefully then pushed the door fully open and
walked to his right. The first small building he came to
was a blacksmith shop. He had never seen one, but his
father had described them to him and he recognized it
from that. He ducked into the shade. There was no one
there, so he continued to the back of the shop and bumped
into large baskets of charcoal piled against the wall.
Climbing over them, Sid crouched down in a dark corner.

He was too nervous to sleep or even rest. He didn't
know when he might have to jump up and run, so he was
alert. There was shouting and the sounds of running men.
He shut his eyes and pretended that he couldn't be seen.

22

Molly and Cook had finished dripping honey on the last batch of dragon ears and had put them in a basket and covered them with a cloth. Molly was excited to be doing something about finding her son. The prospect of going into Rohn's castle was frightening, but being scared wasn't important. The only thing that mattered was getting Sid back.

She looked for Rotug to help carry the baskets of ears and realized that she hadn't seen or heard him in hours. We'll just have to carry the ears ourselves, she thought. "You take that basket on the table and I'll take these two and we'll see how the men like these ears, Cook."

The old woman laughed and shook her head. "I helped you make these things, but I'm not going into the courtyard with something called dragon ears."

Molly looked at Cook with understanding. She didn't want the woman to be embarrassed. "Thank you for your help, Cook. You stay here, and if the men like these, we'll make more later."

Cook turned to the sink and began to wash pans and bowls. Molly carried the three baskets of dragon ears out of the low doorway and through the great hall.

There was a good deal of activity in the courtyard. There were more people there than she had ever seen before. Even more than had been at her wedding, and that had been a lot. She couldn't make much sense of all the commotion and movement, but she did understand that people were working hard. There were soldiers in half armor practicing something and using long poles to do it with. There were even three knights in full armor standing and waiting for their grooms to get their horses ready. It was hard for Molly to understand what was happening, for she had never seen knights before. There was one knight in a kind of harness who was hanging by a chain to a pole that was balanced on a post, and three men on the other end of the pole were pushing down and this was lifting the knight into the air. When he was about eight feet off the ground, one of the grooms led a horse under him. The three on the end of the pole lowered him into his saddle. The knight unhooked the chain and rode off, and another knight stepped up to be put on his horse. What strange things men are, Molly thought.

When the three knights had been put on their horses, Molly carried her baskets over to the group standing by the post. "Would you men like to try some dragon ears?" she asked. The men didn't hear her or didn't care, for they ignored her. Molly nudged one man with her elbow and said, "I made these," and she nodded at the baskets. The man turned away.

This won't do. I'll have to think of some way to get them to try these ears or I won't know if they'll sell to Rohn's men. She looked around and didn't see anything that might help or anyone who was showing any interest in her at all. Now what?

Molly put the baskets on the ground and sat down next to them, spreading her long dress out like a tablecloth. She pulled the cloths away from the ears and exposed them and began eating one. She was paying no attention to the men. She was engrossed in eating and was obviously enjoying it very much. She would take a small bite, put the ear down and lick her fingers carefully and take another bite. Soon there were men standing over her watching her eat. When she had finished the first ear, she hummed to herself, much as Sid did when he liked something he was eating, and she started on her second one.

"What you got there, woman?" one of the men asked.

Molly looked up at him, but didn't answer. She continued to eat, obviously enjoying the ears.

"I said, what are you eating? It looks like cakes or thin bread. Why such small loaves?"

Now Molly could hear other men talking near her.

"What's she sitting on the ground for?"

"What's going on here?"

"Do I smell fresh bread, and why's it smell so good?"

"I asked you, woman, what you got there?" the first man asked again.

This time Molly looked up at him. She smiled around a mouthful of ear and said, "What?"

"You heard me. What's that you're eating?"

"Molly looked around to be sure the other men were looking at her and would be able to hear what she said. "They're dragon ears."

"What?"

"What are they called?"

"Did you hear her?"

There was now a small crowd of men and even a couple of women around Molly. She looked comfortable sitting in the dust of the courtyard eating dragon ears. "I said I'm eating dragon ears," she said loudly.

"They for sale?" asked one of the men.

She shook her head.

"They must be good," another said. "That's the third one I seen her eat."

"Can I have one?" asked one of the women.

Molly stood and brushed the dust off her dress. Picking up one of the baskets, she said, "You may all try them. They're called dragon ears. Help yourselves."

The men and women crowded close, pushing and reaching into the baskets. She could hear sounds of eating and words forced out around ears.

"Good."

"Hey, these are all right."

"Sweet, too."

One of the women said, "Must be honey."

"What is this called?"

Molly laughed and yelled out, "Dragon ears. They're called dragon ears. Do you like them?"

Molly had her answer. The ears would sell at Rohn's castle.

Rotug's people lived near the sea and made their living by sailing to other lands and raiding towns, stealing food and making slaves of children. The children they traded for food with other raiders along the coast.

All of the men in Rotug's country were sailors and could steer by the stars and the sun. Rotug knew which direction to sail to get home, and by the next afternoon the small boat was being pounded by the surf below the hills of his home beach.

The fisherman yelled over the sounds of the waves that were crashing all around them, "We can't land here, it's too rough."

Rotug was hanging onto the tiller, steering the boat between two tall rocks in a line of huge stones that lay just at the surf line. The waves were pounding against them and the spray was like heavy rain on their faces. The fishermen was seated in the bottom of the boat, hanging onto the mast with one hand and bailing as fast as he could with the other. He was using a small wooden bucket without a handle and was having trouble lifting it one-handed over the side of the boat.

"Give bucket to Rotug," the huge man yelled over the noise of the wind and waves. Leaning toward Rotug, the fisherman passed the bucket to him. Rotug held the tiller with one hand and bailed with the other. He had no trouble lifting the full bucket over the side. Soon the bottom of the boat was mostly free of water. All this time Rotug kept his eyes on the huge stones and boulders that were between them and the beach.

Once past those stones they entered the breakers, large waves cresting as they drove toward the shallows near shore. These waves were much higher than the top of the mast, and when they were in the troughs of the waves, they could not see the land at all. But, when the little boat fought to the tops of the crests, Rotug could see his homeland and knew exactly where to steer to make landing.

Past the breakers the water was much calmer. Even the wind seemed to scream less that it had when it had been tossing the tops of the waves over their boat.

When they could feel the bottom scrape on the stones of the beach, both men jumped out, and Rotug pulled the boat clear of the water. He looked for the mark of high tide and made sure the boat would be above that point. After tying the anchor rope to a log that was mostly buried in the stones, he said to the fisherman, "You stay by boat," and smiled when he said, "and guard."

The man nodded as if Rotug's request had been a reasonable one. He took his position near the bow of the boat as Rotug took his huge, double-bladed axe and walked from the beach. After the shale and small stones at the waterline, the beach was covered by fine white sand and long grasses. The blond giant disappeared over the crest of the first dune but came into view again as he reached to top of the next one, and when he had passed over the top, the fisherman didn't see him again.

This time when Axel and Sidney entered the hallway that led to King Willard's rooms, the guard recognized them. "Prince Axel, the king was awake a moment ago. One of his knights just left. Hurry and you might talk with him."

Sidney and Axel quickly crossed the large room and found the king awake. They could hear his faint voice ask, "Who is there?"

"Sidney, the wizard, Your Majesty. And I've brought Axel with me."

The old man tried to sit up, but he was too weak and settled back onto the pillows. But he smiled when he asked, "Axel? My son has come to see me die? How good this is." He held out a shaking hand toward the side of the bed. Axel had to go around the foot of the bed to that side to take the pale and quivering hand.

He was surprised and saddened at how thin and weak the king's hand felt, the skin cool and dry like old paper. "Not to see you die, Your Majesty. Never that."

The king's fingers felt over Axel's hand like he couldn't get enough of the feeling of Axel's skin. He had turned his head toward Axel's voice, but it was obvious that he couldn't see out of his cloudy eyes. They moved in their sockets but didn't settle on Axel's face.

Axel could feel the frail hand pulling him toward the bed and the king said, "Axel, call me Father."

Axel remembered when the king had first asked him to call him Father. At that time he had told King Willard that he wouldn't feel comfortable calling him Father, but now he didn't think it would bother him nearly as much. The pictures he had in his mind of his own father had mostly faded into a general impression that was no longer clear. He placed his other hand over the handful of the king's bones he already was holding.

"I've come because a messenger came to my valley and told me that I was needed here. . .Father."

The king's dry lips smiled slightly. Axel could feel the thin fingers twitch between his hands like a broken-winged bird, frightened and in pain.

The king's voice was as thin as his fingers when he said, "I knew you would come, Son. I had Sidney send for you." He seemed to settle even further into the pillows as if the effort of speaking had exhausted him.

Sidney and Axel waited for some time as the king gathered enough strength to speak again. The old man took in a gulp of air and whispered, "You must save us, Son. Rohn wants the kingdom. You must stop him." Again the king disappeared back into the mattress. Axel could feel the king's hand quiver and twitch.

Axel's throat felt tight and his eyes filled with tears as he said, "Father, I will do whatever it takes to save the kingdom, I promise you this."

After speaking, Axel was surprised that he'd made such a rash promise. He wasn't sure that he even meant it. There were things that were more important to him than the kingdom. He knew that if it meant the kingdom or his family, he'd choose, without hesitation, his family.

Sidney, too, was surprised that Axel had said such a thing. But, Axel was a knight and was pledged to serve his king. This meant that he had to honor all of his promises, especially ones to his king.

Axel felt the frail hand relax and he placed it on the top of the blanket opposite the king's other hand. He turned and looked at Sidney. Sidney nodded his head, and the two men walked quietly to the door.

"Axel, you sure cut down our options here."

"Options?"

"Choices, then."

"Oh, I know the word, but I didn't ever think we had choices. I know I never had any. I have to get Sid back. I don't have any options about that."

"But now you have another one. Your promise to save the kingdom."

"Right." Axel stopped in the dim hallway and thought for a moment before he spoke. "If a person has two things that he's promised to do, he has to do one of them first. This doesn't mean that the second one he keeps is not being kept. . . . Does that make sense?"

Sidney studied Axel's face for a long time. It was almost as if he were trying to read Axel's mind. Finally he nodded and said, "You're right, Axel. You can't do two things at one time any more than anybody else can. Once we save the kingdom we can go back to looking for Sid." Sidney watched Axel's reaction to this like he had been testing Axel and wanted to know how he'd respond.

Axel's voice was hard as he said, "Since I'm the one who has two things that have to be done, Sidney, I'll be the one who decides which one will be done first." Axel turned and continued down the hallway.

Sidney caught up with him at the top of the stairs and said, "You're right, Axel. You have to be the one to choose. I'll support you whichever way you decide to go."

Axel said, "There's no deciding, Sidney. We save Sid before we do anything else."

Sidney said in a voice too low for Axel to hear, "I wish for you both at the same time, my friend."

25

Molly returned to the king's kitchen with two empty baskets. She had been pleased that the people of the castle liked them so much. For the first time she felt positive about doing something to find her son.

No one questioned her when she carried the third basket to the large door that had been lowered over the moat, and this surprised her. Maybe it was because there were other people leaving the castle at the same time and the guard thought she worked here.

Some of the men recognized her and smiled and looked at the basket she was carrying. One short woman walked next to her on the long neck of land that led to the road to Willardville. Over her dress she was wearing a long and darkly stained apron. Her face looked pushed together, and when she spoke, Molly could see this was because she had lost her teeth. This didn't seem to bother or embarrass her when she pointed to the cloth covering the basket and asked, "Where did you learn to make dragon ears, dear?"

Molly smiled and said, "My father taught me to make them for the people who stayed at his inn."

"But such a strange name he give them."

Molly smiled but didn't know what to say, and the woman said quickly, "I don't mean no offense by that, Miss."

Molly smiled at her and nodded her head. "It is a strange name, isn't it?"

"Oh, yes. I just wonder how you got it."

"I think Rotug thought it up."

The woman frowned and said, "Rotug? Who's that? I never heard of anybody called anything like Rotug."

Molly felt as if maybe she had made a mistake. She didn't know if she should have talked about Rotug to these people. After all, it had only been a little over a year since Rotug's people had besieged this castle and killed most of the stock in the nearby farms. They wouldn't take kindly to one of the blue men coming back and staying in the castle.

"Molly shrugged her shoulders, smiled and said in an offhand way, "He's just a friend who's travelled a lot." There, she hadn't lied and, if the woman accepted that, the problem wouldn't come up. She'd just have to watch what she said from now on, though.

Molly smiled at the woman again and asked, "Where are the Gypsies camped? Near here?"

They were at the junction where the road led into Willardville. The woman pointed to the far side of the rutted roadway, toward the west and down into a small depression next to a woods. "There. Can you see the colored wagons just this side of those trees?" She gave Molly a moment to look and then went on, "They come every fall and camp there and sell things to the people in the castle and some to the people in town. Some say they take more things away than they leave, though."

Molly studied the small circle of wagons and didn't answer immediately for she didn't understand what the woman was saying. Take away more than they leave. What could that mean? Rather than make herself more noticed than she already was, she said, "I see them. That's where I'm going with this basket of dragon ears. Maybe I can sell them to the Gypsies."

"If you sell them, why'd you give them away this afternoon?"

"I just wanted to see if people would like them."

"But you said that you used to make them for the people in your father's inn. You must know that people like them." The woman was looking intently at Molly now.

I've got to do something about this conversation with this woman, Molly thought. I can't have people curious about us as long as we have Rotug with us. And another thing, there could even be one of Rohn's spies in the castle, and it would be bad if he heard about strange people in Amory with something called dragon ears. I have to think of something to get her mind off me and Rotug. She smiled at the woman and asked, "Do you work in the castle for the king?"

The woman didn't answer right away, just looked at Molly, and her eyes traveled over her face much the way blind people move their fingers over people's faces when they first meet them. This made Molly uncomfortable. What to say? How to say it? What to do? She wished that Axel were here, but she was alone.

No. She didn't need Axel. She had a very small problem, and she could solve it herself. If she was going to be a spy she had to be able to handle herself better than she had so far with this woman.

"What I mean is, I'd think it would be exciting working in a huge castle like that. My husband and I travel from place to place, and I'd like for us to live in just one place." There, that wasn't a lie. "I gave the dragon ears away to see if the people in the castle would like them. If they did, that would mean that I might be able to sell them to people living in a castle. It was. . .a market experience."

The woman relaxed and started to nod her head but stopped and said, "Market experience? I never heard of that before, either."

Molly thought of Sidney and his experiments. She had heard him one time call what he did "research."

"Market research. I'm sure you know what that is," she said and took a dragon ear from the basket and handed it to the woman.

The woman smiled and said, "Oh, thank you, Miss. I never got one in the courtyard when you was giving them away. Now I'll know what they taste like," and she tore a large piece off and shoved it into her mouth. Around the mouthful of ear, she said, "This's good. You should be able to sell them easy. I heard people that already had some say the same. Your market research works just fine."

They were friends now and Molly could relax again as she turned off the road and followed a track to the wagons near the woods.

26

When Sid next opened his eyes, he could see patches of lighter shadows and knew that morning had come. It was still early for there were no noises of people moving or working, but there was a gray light in the opening of the blacksmith shop.

After he had climbed over the baskets of charcoal and stood in the center of the shop, he saw that he was well covered with black charcoal dust. He pounded his hands against his clothes, but that caused clouds of dust to swirl around him. He could feel the grit of it in his mouth and his eyes stung.

A bucket of water sat next to the forge and Sid drank some then washed his hands and splashed it over his face.

He was looking for a rag to wipe off with and had his back to the open front of the shop when a loud voice said, "Brought more charcoal, did you, Boy? Good for you. I like a boy starts the day early."

Sid was startled by the voice, and, when he turned to face the man, he found he was right next to him. He had to look almost straight up to see his face. The blacksmith is about as old as my father, he thought. But he's almost as big as Rotug.

"Not only at work early but not a talker, either. Good for you, Boy. I could use a boy like you here to help me. Looking to be an apprentice to a blacksmith?"

It wasn't that Sid was too scared to speak; he didn't know what to say. Of course, he couldn't work for this man. People would see him and know he didn't belong here.

Sid was about to say that he wasn't bringing charcoal and didn't want work when he thought, How can I explain

99

my being here in this man's shop? I sure don't want to lie, but maybe I can avoid saying things that aren't true.

"Do you have work for someone as small as me, Sir?"

The huge man laughed and said, "There's nobody else to help, they all been put in the army. Somebody else will have to deliver the charcoal." He pointed to the back of the shop and said, "Your job for now is to keep the fire good and hot. You got to bring charcoal up here and keep the furnace full, and you got to keep it hot when I need to heat iron. You pump here on these bellows when I tell you to. Think you can remember that?"

This man must think I'm dumb, Sid thought. "Yes, Sir. I can remember to do those things. Is that all you want of me?"

"For now it is. Here, tie this around your face to cover your nose and mouth. Keep the dust out." He handed Sid a rag. As Sid was tying it around his head, the man asked, "You had food yet?"

Did that sound good. "No, Sir."

"You come with me and we'll find you something to keep your fire going." The large man grinned and Sid thought that all the people in this castle might not be as mean as the first ones he'd met.

27

On that same dawn, Sidney met Axel in the king's kitchen. This time Cook acted like she was glad to see them. She hurried as quickly as she was able to putting hard boiled eggs, bread and a pot of butter on the table. The men filled tin cups with water at the well in the corner of the room.

While they were eating, Sidney asked, "What did Molly learn from making all those dragon ears?"

Axel was spooning porridge into his mouth. He stopped and said, "She said the people here in the castle liked them. And she took some to that band of Gypsies camped near the woods. They liked them, too."

"You going to let her join them, Axel?"

Axel looked at his hands and thought before he replied, "I don't think I have a whole lot to say about it. She's made up her mind and she'll do what she thinks might help get Sid back."

Sidney said, "That whole thing sounds dangerous to me. There she is in Rohn's castle, surrounded by his army, she's alone and Rohn would love to have both Sid and her. I know you have to do what you think's best, but this worries me."

"It worries me, too, Sidney, but you don't know Molly like I do. . . . I guess I don't know Molly like I like I thought I did either." Axel shook his head and continued, "I don't like Molly being in danger, but if I said she couldn't go. . .she might go anyway. And, if she didn't go, we both might regret it."

Sidney studied his friend's face and said, "I think I understand what you mean," He nodded and went on, "Right, we have our own problems to solve. Let's check on the blacksmith this morning. See how he's coming with the canon."

"We named it a cavgon, not a canon, Sidney."

"Whatever it's called, lets see how he's doing with it."

The two friends heard the sound of iron being beaten as soon as they were through the outside doorway of the great room. The courtyard was still fairly dark but they could see that it was empty. Because he was lit by the fire glowing in his forge, they could see the blacksmith working in a shop that looked as if it had been built into the far wall of the castle.

The sky had cleared in the night and there was a brisk wind blowing the flags stiffly to the north. Indeed, the air was much warmer, and Axel felt better about everything right away. Maybe Molly will find out where Sid is, maybe the cavgon will work and toss pots at Rohn's men. Although what good that would do he couldn't imagine.

As they walked across the courtyard, Axel asked, "Sidney, what good will it do to have a cavgon that tosses clay pots at Rohn's soldiers?" Axel held his hands out from his side and continued, "Even if a pot hits someone, they're not heavy enough to hurt. All it'll do is confuse them and maybe make them mad. I don't understand this at all."

Axel stopped talking and watched his friend's face. Sidney didn't react. He was looking straight ahead toward the blacksmith's shop. Axel said, "Why don't you tell me what you're thinking? You always have before."

"What I'll do is show you exactly what I've been thinking as soon as I can get all the things together. I don't think you'll be disappointed, Axel."

The blacksmith was working with a strip of iron about as wide as Axel's thumb. Sidney and Axel watched as the big man heated a section of the strip of flattened iron, and while it was still soft from the heat, he slid it over a short log the size of the pot he'd been given. Pounding on the heated section and holding the log on the anvil, he was able to wrap another turn of the strip tightly around the log. Axel could see that the strip he was working with was long enough that the log would be completely covered by the strip when he was finished.

He slid out the now smoking log and placed the section just past the first bend into the coals and heated it again until it glowed bright orange in the dim shop and then wrestled it back onto the anvil. After he had rein-serted the log, he pounded it tightly around the smoking wood. When the man looked up, Sidney asked, "How do you know how strong to make it?"

The blacksmith laid his hammer down and turning toward Sidney, said, "I don't."

Axel touched Sidney on the arm to get his attention and said, "It has to be stronger than the body of a dragon, Sidney."

Sidney continued to watch the blacksmith for a short while as he resumed work, and finally responded by frowning and turned to look at Axel and asked, "What?"

"You remember what happened to the dragons when they blew up, don't you?" Axel asked.

"Sure, they died." Sidney pointed to the short log almost completely covered in the wrapping of iron and said, "Are you worried about the cavgon dying, Axel?"

"No. The dragons blew up all over the cave. That was just pieces of meat and bones. Think what it would be like if the cavgon blew up like that. There'd be pieces of iron flying in all directions."

Sidney raised his eyebrows, turned back to the anvil, and Axel saw his lips moving and his head nodding as if he were talking to someone. Finally he looked at Axel and then at the blacksmith and said, "Hold on there a bit, blacksmith. What are you going to do with that to make it strong? We don't want it coming apart on us."

"How strong ya want it?"

Sidney thought for a moment and said, "I don't know."

The large man wiped the sweat from his face and said as he smiled, "I think that it's about that strong now. It may be almost done."

Axel didn't understand what these two men were saying to each other. If Sidney didn't know. . .the thing is that strong now. . .How could the man know. . . ?"

"Let's have him make it a bit stronger than that, Sidney," Axel said.

Sidney leaned over the anvil and examined the cavgon carefully. "Could we wrap it once more the other way?"

"I can wrap it as many times as ya want me to, but ya got to tell me what ya want, Wizard."

"I want it wrapped again with the strips going around the log in the opposite direction."

Sidney turned to Axel and asked, "What do you think, Axel? That do it?"

"That depends on what you want it to do."

Sidney turned back to the blacksmith and said, "Wrap it one more time and that will be fine, Blacksmith. You remember that we have to have a small hole in the covered end?"

The large man looked at the wall where they had drawn the picture of the cavgon and said, "Ya drew a picture. I can make anything ya can draw. I'll have this ready for ya by tomorrow morning," and he turned and began to pump the bellows. The charcoal glowed and sent up a shower of sparks which filled the small shop with smoke and soot. He slid the smoking log out of the wrapping and slung the metal over to the fire and thrust the end into the bright coals.

When they were standing in the morning sunlight again, Sidney said, "We should check on the potter and see how the pots are coming along." He looked at the sky and continued, "It's still early enough so that we could get to the cave yet today."

"What cave?"

"The one with the peppers in it, of course."

Axel turned away and headed for the entrance to the great room. "I have to talk to Molly if she's up. I want to know what she plans on doing with those dragon ears."

"That can wait. I need you with me today, Axel."

"What for? You can look at the pots by yourself, and I'm sure not going down into a cave full of hot peppers and dragon eggs."

Sidney looked at his friend and thought of what he could say that would get Axel to help him. "I need you, Axel."

"What about the eggs?"

"What eggs?"

"You know what I'm talking about. We didn't use anywhere near all the eggs on the blue men. There must have been over a hundred left in the cave."

Sidney scuffed his boot in the dust of the courtyard and said in a very low voice, "I never counted them all."

Axel reached over and pulled on Sidney's sleeve, causing Sylvia to wobble on his shoulder, and said, "You have to know." When Sidney had steadied his pet, he looked at Axel and said, "What?"

Knowing that Sidney had heard him, Axel just looked at his friend.

Sidney said in a much louder voice, "I don't know how many there were in the cave. I don't see how it matters."

"You have a hundred rotten dragon eggs and a huge pile of dried peppers in the same cave and you don't think it matters? Sidney, this is crazy." Axel raised his voice almost to a shout. "Sid is gone and you want to play at making scrambled eggs and peppers?"

Sidney's voice took an indigent tone when he said, "I"m not playing, this is research."

"Well great. You research and I'll find Molly."

Sidney held Axel's arm and said, "I need your thinking, Axel. You have the best ideas of any man I ever met, and we have a better chance of getting Sid back if we work together. It's what Molly wants. She's planning on going to Rohn's castle to see if she can learn where Sid is, and we have to come up with ideas about how we can stop Rohn's army."

Sidney lowered the volume of his voice and continued, "I know you don't want to be involved in any killing." He held his arms out to the side and said, "If the cavgon works, nobody needs to die and we can stop Rohn. Maybe, if we know where Sid is we can even figure out a way to get him without killing anyone."

That was a long speech for the wizard, and Axel was impressed with it. Maybe Sidney was right. Molly certainly was a lot more forceful than he had thought she was. He was both surprised and just a little annoyed by the whole idea of her making decisions without regard to what he thought and then acting on them whether he wanted her to or not.

He, of course, was proud of her. He knew that she loved Sid as much as he did and wanted him back just as strongly, but, still. . . . Some things are done by men and women have no place in them at all. Dealing with kidnappers has to be men's work. Women don't get involved in evil things or plots or in planning actions against enemies. Those things are done by men and that's the way it should be.

Still, Molly has her rights as a mother to do what has to be done to protect her family. Just because things have always been done by men doesn't mean that they always have to be in the future.

But, Molly wasn't the typical woman, either. That's why he loved her so much. She was special. Maybe part of being special was wanting to do things on her own. Axel felt both a sense of loss of control and a pride in his wife making her own decisions. But he had to be careful that this didn't become a habit.

Think what life would be like if, when they all got back to the valley, she still wanted to make decisions and insisted on running things outside of the kitchen. He'd have to worry about that when he had more time.

28

The potter's shop was on the other side of the courtyard, and the woman was at her wheel working when Axel and Sidney arrived. She looked up to see who had blocked her light, then continued stroking the heavy bottom wheel with the ball of her foot. She dipped her fingers in a bowl of water, then using her palms, shaped the lump of clay turning in the center of the top wheel.

The heavy bottom wheel, acting as a flywheel, and the lighter top wheel were both on the same shaft. The turning of the wheels made a sound similar to one made by a spinning wheel, but it was heavier or lower in pitch and very constant.

The potter was seated close to the top wheel and didn't have to reach to push the bottom one with her bare foot. The turning bottom wheel kept the top wheel rotating at a constant speed, which she needed to work the clay.

Axel was fascinated by what she was doing. He had used clay bowls even as a child, but he had never even thought about how they were made. He had thought that someone started with a lump of clay and carefully shaped it. Watching how this woman did it, he realized that this would be the only way to get the shape really round. What a wonderful idea.

When the bowl was the general shape the woman wanted, she measured the hole in the top with a wooden cork by placing the cork gently in the hole. She worked with the clay, pulling it toward the hole until the cork would fit tightly.

She then measured the size of the pot by holding a thin board with a section cut out of it up against the pot. When the pot just fit into the cut out section, she knew that it was the right size. That must be the size of the inside of the cavgon, Axel thought.

When she was finished with the pot she was working on, she cut it from the wheel with a piece of string. After smoothing the bottom of the pot, she set it aside with some others, Sidney said, "You've been working hard. They look good. What do they look like after you cook them?"

She smiled and said, "I don't cook 'em. I fire 'em to make the clay hard."

"Same thing," Sidney said.

"No it's not," she said in low a voice, as she scratched her skin just below her throat, leaving a gray smudge of clay.

"Is too."

"Is not."

Sidney nodded his head.

The potter shook hers.

Axel shouted, "What are you doing, Sidney? We've got important things to do and you're playing games."

Sidney glanced at Axel and said just loud enough for him to hear, "Same."

The woman glanced at Axel and very slightly shook her head.

Sidney examined the pots that had been fired and nodded his head. "These look good. But, we may need more of them than I thought."

"You said twenty."

"We may need more."

Speaking now with some impatience, she said, "I made nineteen up now. I got one more to make and that's your twenty."

"We may require more than twenty."

The woman stood beside the wheel and, looking into Sidney's face, said, "You said twenty,"

"That was yesterday."

"That's what you said, twenty." She pointed to the row of pots on a shelf. "I made twenty."

Sidney smiled and nodded his head when he said, "And today we may need more than twenty."

She said softly, "Twenty yesterday."

Sidney said just as softly, "Another twenty more today."

Axel again yelled. "Sidney, stop this."

Sidney turned and left the shop and Axel had to hurry to keep up with him. He could just hear Sidney saying under his breath, "More today."

After they had saddled their horses, they rode out of the gate into the still, early morning. The mist had burned off the top of the cliff but still hung over the water so that the horizon was hidden. The trees along the coast lost their leaves earlier than the ones in his valley did. Strange. Maybe it was the wind from the sea that did it. In any event, it was a warm morning and Axel looked forward to a fine fall day.

The ride to the chimney was familiar to both men, for it was there that they had trained the twin dragons to drop the dragon eggs on a blue cloth. Before noon they were at the chimney cave.

This was the first time Axel had seen the whole chimney, for there had always been fog or mist in the depression. In this low piece of ground ringed with woods was the tall circular rock that was the entrance to the dragon's cave. Wind and water had weathered it so that the surface was rough and layered and easy to climb.

The first time Axel had seen the chimney rock, he hadn't known if the dragon was inside the cave or out feeding. He'd meant to make a quick descent into the cave, pound the chained hooks into the walls and wait for the dragon to return and find him there. He had learned that dragons can communicate, and he'd felt that this dragon had learned that he would be able to kill her only if she tried to burn him with her fire.

He'd hoped that this dragon would impale her tail on the hooks, get frustrated and try to use her fire to kill him. That was the only time that he could kill one of the beasts. It had worked that way with the first three dragons he'd met. That had been the last one in the kingdom and he had to know because he'd been betting his life on the hooks.

He felt relief that this time, as they climbed the rock, for there was no dragon waiting for them in the blackness of the cave. Sidney carried a lantern and Axel the rope they'd to use to drop down the mouth of the chimney.

He tied one end of the rope around the top of the chimney and dropped the other end into the black hole. He heard the thud when it hit the stone floor. Sidney tied the lantern to his belt and lowered himself down the rope. Axel followed, and by the time he felt the stones of the floor with his boots, the lantern was casting Sidney's shape on the walls of the dim room below ground.

Axel glanced over his head at the small circle of light that was the top of the chimney then turned and entered the main part of the cave. Sidney was standing by a pile of brush and asked, "This's where you found the egg, isn't it, Axel?" His voice sounded dead and muffled.

Axel remembered the excitement he'd felt when he'd realized that the rubbery ball he'd held in his hands was a dragon's egg. It had been just then that the female dragon had returned and sat on the top of the chimney, blocking off both the light and his only escape route.

Axel pointed to the center of the large pile of brush and said, "Right there. Now where are these peppers, Sidney?"

"They're over here," Sidney said, as he walked to the far wall of the cave.

When Axel followed him, he saw, not the wall of the cave, but the wall of dragon eggs that he remembered from a year ago. They gleamed a dull green in the yellow light.

Axel was amazed. He'd assumed that Sidney would bury them or something, not leave them where someone might stumble onto them. They were really dangerous. He remembered how the blue men had rolled on the ground and retched and held their sides when they'd been splattered with the rotten eggs.

"They're still here, Sidney?"

"Sure, I only brought them here last year," Sidney said, pointing to a waist-high pile of dark brown peppers.

"No, Sidney. You know I mean the eggs."

Sidney held his hands away from his body and said, "Good place for them, Axel. They're underground. It's cool. They haven't broken open. Nobody knows they're here, so it's safe.

Axel stared at his friend and shook his head. This wasn't like Sidney. He had always been careful of hurting other people, and yet, he had left these eggs here in this cave. . . . But, maybe this isn't such a bad place. Out of sight, not easy to get to, away from the heat and sun so they won't burst open and nobody knows they're here. This might be all right, after all.

"What about the peppers, Sidney? What are you going to do with them?"

Sidney walked to where Axel was standing and, looking down at the pile of dried peppers, said, "We're going to grind them up and fill the pots with them."

"So we have twenty pots full of pepper dust?"

"Sure. But forty.

"Forty?"

"You remember that I told the potter to make twenty more?"

That conversation came back to Axel. He looked closely at Sidney and said, "And?"

"And then when we have to, we blast them at Rohn's men."

"With the cavgon, right?"

"Sure."

Axel turned and grabbed the rope and began to pull himself up the shaft. "That's crazy, Sidney. I have to find Molly."

Sidney ran to the end of the rope and yelled, "Wait, Axel. Give me a chance to tell you how this'll work."

Axel dropped back to the floor of the cave and faced his friend.

"The pots have a hole in them, right?"

Shaking his head with impatience, Axel said, "Right."

"We have dried peppers that are very powerful if they get on someone's skin or they breathe them in, right?"

Axel didn't say anything and Sidney just looked at him, waiting. Finally Axel gave in and said, "Right."

"We could put the peppers in the pots and something could be put in the holes to keep them there, right?"

Axel nodded his head.

"The cavgon could blast the pots out to where Rohn's men are and drive them away, right?"

Axel turned and again grabbed the rope.

"No, Axel. You have to work with me on this. What are you going to do to get Sid back even if Molly can find out where he is?"

Axel dropped the rope and said, "I don't know that."

Sidney shrugged his shoulders and looked away.

Axel was quiet while he thought of what he could do if he knew where Rohn was keeping Sid. He couldn't think of anything. This plan of Sidney's was crazy but it was a plan, and he didn't even have that much. This couldn't work but just maybe. . . .

"All right, Sidney. How do we get the peppers ground up and in the pots?"

"Now that's a problem, isn't it?"

Axel waited.

Sidney was still for a bit and Axel could see his lips work as he talked to himself. When he was ready, he said, "We take the peppers up to a large flat rock. We tie a rope around another rock and drag it over the peppers and it grinds them up."

"That might work," Axel said. The two men were now sitting in the place where Sidney had had them sit when he'd introduced Axel to the twin dragons. Axel remembered looking into the black slits of the yellow eyes of the first of the twins. It was close enough to his face that he could feel the warmth of its breath on his skin, and he saw again the black snake-like tongue as it flicked out and almost touched his face.

"And how do we get the peppers in the pots?"

"I'm still working on that, Axel."

"We do this one step at a time, is that it?"

"Sure. Let's get the peppers out of here and find a place to grind them up."

"Let's get the pots here first."

Sidney looked surprised and said. "Sorry. I got carried away, Axel. Of course, we have to get the pots first." Sidney crossed the small cave to the rope and started up the shaft.

29

Axel had insisted they stop at the grove where the Gypsies camped, but when they got there the wagons were gone, the ground muddy and rutted with wheel marks.

Axel stood in the road and looked to the north toward Rohn's castle and imagined Molly walking toward him. He didn't understand what had happened. He had been happy living in a beautiful valley with his family. He had everything he had dreamed of and had worked hard to get, but it had all disappeared.

His son had been kidnapped by someone and was being held hostage. His wife had gone looking for him with a band of Gypsies. His king was dying and he was supposed to be the next king and he didn't want that at all. Everything that had been so wonderful was now gone. What had he done wrong or what had he done to deserve this?

The pots were ready when they returned to the potter's shop the next morning. Sidney met Axel there after packing the things they'd need to load the peppers into the pots. When the potter showed them the twenty pots she'd made, Sidney told her the king really did need twenty more. The woman shook her head and Axel heard her say, "Twenty on one day and another twenty on the next day. What are you gonna want for tomorrow?"

"Twenty more?" Sidney said as he put one of the pots in a pouch in his cloak.

Axel turned and looked back at the woman as they were leaving the shop. Her eyes had already disappeared in the darkness of her face, but he could see her lips moving as she continued the conversation with Sidney.

Axel and Sidney crossed the courtyard to the blacksmith's shop. The large man was bending over the cavgon at the front of the shop. Axel was as surprised as Sidney was to see that it had two wheels on a frame that looked like it came from a wheelbarrow. The blacksmith grinned a welcome when they stopped outside his shop to watch him center the cavgon in the entrance. "What ya think now?" he said, his hands on his hips and his shoulders thrown back with pride.

Sidney knelt in the dirt and examined the cavgon. He ran his hands over the closely packed turnings of the bands of iron. He looked for and found the hole in the end where they were going to put fire to the firestarter material inside. After Sidney had looked down the barrel he turned and, looking up at Axel, said, "This is wonderful, Axel. We can put it anywhere we want to."

"But, why do we need the wheels?" Axel asked.

The blacksmith said, "Ya need em. It was too heavy for me to carry around, and whatever you're gonna use it for, you'll have to move it sometimes. Ya need wheels."

Axel saw the sense of that and was pleased with the looks of Sidney's new toy. He doubted that it'd work the way Sidney said it would, but he was willing to find out. "How's it going to work, Sidney?"

Sidney glanced at Axel to catch his eye then looked at the blacksmith. "I'll show you later, Axel. He looked at the blacksmith and said, "There's one more thing the king needs, Blacksmith."

The large man nodded and said, "Can ya draw it?"

Sidney drew on the wall and Axel was surprised at how real the picture looked. Sidney he drew a picture of a strangely shaped funnel. It had a large apron on one side of the wide end. He talked as he drew. "This can be

117

made out of very thin metal, even thinner than the stuff that you make cooking pans out of. The small end of the funnel has to be just a bit smaller than the hole in this pot," he said, digging the pot out of his cloak.

"When's the king want it?"

"About an hour will do us nicely, Blacksmith."

"Ya come back in an hour and I'll have it for ya," the blacksmith said, turning toward the back of his shop.

Sidney said, "Let's get Winthton and figure how to hook up the cavgon. By then the blacksmith should be done." He gave the cavgon a kick and acted surprised that it didn't move. Sidney turned toward the courtyard and limped his way to the stable.

It was easy hitching Winthton to the cavgon. They used the tack designed for pulling a plow. It was perfect, and very soon they had the cavgon ready to travel. By the time they finished, the blacksmith was watching them with the funnel in his hand. When they saw him, he said, "This is what ya asked for," and he held it out.

Sidney turned it slowly in his hands and said, "This is exactly what I. . .er. . .the king had in mind."

The large man frowned and said, "I don't know what ya. . .er. . .the king had in mind, but that's what ya drew on the wall. I can make what ya draw."

Sidney fitted the end of the funnel into the hole in the pot, and looking at Axel said, "It fits, Axel."

Sounding cross, the blacksmith said in a loud voice, "A' course, it fits. It's what ya asked for."

"Thanks, Blacksmith," Sidney said, as he found a place on the cavgon to hang the funnel. The two men stopped in the kitchen before they left the castle. They might be more than one day so they had decided to ask Cook to pack them some food.

30

The next morning the wind was again cold and blowing winter ahead of it, the sound mixing with crashing of the waves. Axel had heard the uneven rhythm most of the way to the cave—the waves pounding and pounding against huge stones, the pieces that had broken away and fallen to the water at the base of the cliff.

It was slow traveling this morning because the wheels on the cavgon were so close together that it tipped on its side when it hit a rut in the road. And the frozen road was very badly rutted and the ruts were hard.

They had ridden with their cloaks pulled tightly around themselves and had alternated hands on the reins, so that they could keep one hand inside their cloaks.

Just before Sidney put his foot on the edge of the chimney, Axel took hold of Sidney's arm and said, "Before we go back down there, Sidney, I have to know what we're going to do."

"Don't you trust me, my boy?"

"Sure, I do. But. . .I want to know."

Sidney took a large breath and said around the frost, "First we're going to test the cavgon to see how far it'll throw the pots. We'll bring up some peppers, grind them up and pack them in the pots."

"Good, thanks, Sidney. Now, how are you going to do that to the peppers without getting burned?"

Sidney looked into Axel's face and smiled. He said, "I thought I'd leave that part of this to you, Axel. You have to do your part, you know."

"No. I'm not going to touch them," Axel said.

"You won't have to. I'll do that part."

Axel stopped. "You sure?"

"Sure. Now help me fill this test pot with sand."

Sidney set the pot on the rocky ground and wedged stones against its sides. When it seemed secure to him he stuck the small end of the funnel in the hole and said, "Here, Axel, hold this while I pour in the sand."

"Sure, I will, but I don't understand what you're doing. Sand isn't going to hurt anyone."

"I can't do it by myself. It may not be fun but we're working to get Sid back, you know."

Axel felt shame that Sidney had to reminded him of that. Sidney didn't have to do any of this. It was all for Sid. And here he was being reluctant to help as much as he could. He said, "Sorry, Sidney. You're right, I'll hold it while you pour." Axel held the funnel upright and Sidney dribbled sand into the wide apron. The wind caught the first handful, and blew some of it away. Sidney had to shield the funnel with his other hand.

"We might have to do this part in the cave, Axel."

When Sidney had put in three handfuls he said, "That ought to be enough for the test, wouldn't you think, Axel?" He looked up at his friend.

"About three handfuls for each one of Rohn's men."

Sidney stood with the pot in his hand and began stuffing a rag in the hole. "You don't want to test the cavgon with a pot full of pepper, do you?"

Of course that's what Sidney was doing. He had to see what happened when he put fire to the cavgon, and he didn't want to take a chance with a pot of pepper. When he answered, Axel had respect in his voice for the first time. "You're right. I hadn't thought of that."

They had brought Winthton with the cavgon down into the depression near the chimney. Sidney set the funnel and pot on the ground and took the pack from Winthton's back and opened it on a level spot next to them. Axel realized for the first time that Winthton's pack must have the firestarter powder in it.

Sidney was very careful when he opened the bag of firestarter material. Again he asked Axel to hold the funnel. Axel looked at the small end of the funnel and said, "It's too big for that small hole, Sidney." Sidney pointed to the open end of the cavgon. Axel nodded.

Sidney lifted the end of the cavgon, and Axel was surprised that he could do that. Sidney must be stronger than he looks, he thought. On the ride up, it had taken both of them working together to right the cavgon when it tipped over. Axel stuck the funnel in the end of the cavgon and Sidney poured the firestarter powder into the funnel. Shielding the funnel from the wind with his body, he poured until the small bag was empty.

"How do you know how much to use?" asked Axel.

"I don't."

"Well then, How do you know. . . ?

Sidney removed the funnel and stood. He brushed off his hands and said, "This is research, Axel."

"How can this be research?"

"I mean that we have an idea of what we're doing, but we're not real sure how to go about it."

"Is that how you came up with the new stirrup?"

"No, that was experimental research."

"What's the difference?"

Sidney sat with his back against the chimney and patted the still frost-covered ground next to him. Axel sat. "With research you know almost what you're doing and what the result should be. With experimental research, you know what you want to happen, but you don't know how to get it to happen."

It that how you made the firestarter powder?"

"No. That was basic research."

"Basic research?"

"Sure. Basic research is when you don't know what you're doing or why you're doing it or what will happen when you do do it."

Axel shook his head and said, "That's a little confusing, Sidney."

Sidney patted his friend on the arm and said, "That's why I'm a wizard and you're a farmer, Axel."

Axel understood that and said, "That makes sense to me now. Is this cavgon the result of that kind of research?"

"What kind?"

"Basic research."

Sidney thought for a moment and said, "No, this is the result of experimental research," He waved his hand at the equipment. "The *idea* of the cavgon was the result of mental research."

"I don't understand that at all."

Sidney held one hand out in front of him and said, "That's the kind of research a wizard does in his mind."

That didn't help. How could someone do something in his mind? "How does that work, Sidney?"

Sidney counted on his fingers as he explained, "Mental research is when I see that I have a problem. I figure out what will solve the problem for me. I look at what materials or things I have to work with to solve the problem. I list the steps that I'll take to solve it. And, I do all that in my head."

Axel recognized this process for Sidney had taught it to him years ago. He thought for a bit and said, "Now I can see why you didn't try to solve the problem of the wild peppers with mental research."

"Why?

"The peppers would have burned your head."

Sidney looked at Axel for a moment, his face blank. He blinked, stood and said, "Let's eat after we try this."

While Sidney was trying the fit of the pot in the end of the cavgon, Axel examined the small hole the blacksmith had put in the closed end. "How are you going put fire down this little hole?"

"I have no idea."

"Axel was trying to see down the small hole into the barrel where the powder was. "There has to be something in this hole so that when you set it on fire, the fire reaches the rest of the powder, doesn't there?"

"That would be right."

"But you just poured the powder in the end and then you're going to put the pot in on top of it. How do we know that the powder is clear down on this end?"

Sidney gestured with his hands as he started to explain. "You see, when I poured. . .You know, you're right. I don't know where the powder is, and it has to be at that end. This thing is too heavy to pick up and shake. We both might be able to do it, but that can't be the best way."

Axel looked down the big hole in the end of the barrel and said, "It's too small for my hand or I could push the powder down there."

Sidney said, "This is a problem. I think what we have to do is put something in there so we can push the powder all the way to the end. Then, when we put the pot in, it will roll clear down to the where the powder is."

Looking at the woods that surrounded the depression Axel said, "If we could catch a squirrel, that would do it."

"How would that help?"

"We could put the squirrel in the end and push it tight against the powder."

Sidney laughed and said, "That's it, my boy. That's what we'll do."

Axel was alarmed and shouted, "I wasn't serious, Sidney. We can't do that to a small animal."

"Sidney looked at the end of the cavgon and said, "This hole's too small for a big animal."

Axel threw up his arms and shouted, "We can't use any size animal that way."

Sidney was digging in his pack and said, "The idea is right though. We stuff something in the hole and use it to push the powder to the end. We just think squirrel."

He found what he'd been looking for and threw a blue cloth over the end of the cavgon and headed for the woods. "I'll be right back."

Axel recognized the cloth. It was the one they'd used to train the twins to drop eggs on. They'd spread it on the ground and. . . . Axel turned and looked at the spot where he'd stood on the cloth as a dragon flew toward him with a bundle of rags in its claws. He remembered how scared he'd been.

"Here, Axel, this ought to do it." Sidney held a short length of broken limb. He tore off a piece of cloth and stuffed it into the end of the cavgon and pushed it in with the limb. "That should be far enough, Axel."

Next he put the pot in and shoved it to the far end. "Now all we have to do is pour some firestarter powder into the small hole and it's ready for the test." Sidney pulled another bag of powder from his pack and tried to pour powder into the hole. The wind caught the powder and blew if off the top of the cavgon. Very little went into the hole.

Axel said, "We could use a smaller funnel for this."

Looking at his friend, Sidney said, "I think you got it. We'll make a small funnel out of a leaf. See if you can find a big one in the woods that isn't all dried out while I fix up this mess."

By the time Axel returned with a handful of leaves, Sidney had the spilled powder cleaned up and was standing next to the cavgon waiting for him.

Sidney rolled one of the leaves into a cylinder and put one end in the small hole. Using two fingers, he spread the top of the leaf so that he had a crude funnel. "Here, Axel, you hold the funnel while I pour."

The powder went into the hole with no trouble. When the hole was full and there was a small pile of powder setting on the top of the barrel, Sidney dug his firestarter from his pack.

Axel remembered the explosion in Sidney's room and backed up until his back was against the chimney.

"What's the matter, Axel?"

"I think I'll feel better if I'm on the other side of this rock," he said, stepping behind the chimney. He did look around to see what Sidney was doing, though.

Beckoning Axel forward, Sidney said, "You can have the honor of firing the first cavgon ever, Axel."

"No thanks," Axel said from behind the chimney.

Smiling, Sidney said, "You have to have confidence when you do research."

"I have it."

"It doesn't look like it to me."

"I have confidence that you'll light the cavgon."

"It hurts to hear your doubt, Axel," Sidney said as he turned the cavgon so that it was aimed away from the chimney. He wanted to know how far the pot flew.

Sidney stood at the back of the cavgon and sighted along the barrel. When it was pointed just right, he set the firestarter board on top of the cavgon and stuck the flint against the steel set into the board. Sparks but no flame. Again. The wind must be too strong and is blowing the sparks away from the powder, Axel thought.

Axel had just leaned back around the rock and didn't see what happened next, and it was just as good he was protected. There was a tremendous roar, and a singing and whistling, and something hit the chimney hard enough for Axel to feel the impact as he leaned against it.

He looked around the corner, and where Sidney had stood by the cavgon, there was a huge cloud of black smoke and dust. Sidney and the cavgon were hidden. . .or gone. He shouted as he ran into the smoke, "Sidney, are you all right?"

There was no answer, but Axel ran hard into a coughing Sidney and both men fell to the ground. Axel grabbed the first part of Sidney that he could hold on to and dragged him toward the chimney and out of the smoke and dust. "What happened, Sidney? Are you hurt? That was the loudest noise I ever heard, even louder than when the dragons blew up."

Sidney was wiping his eyes and was bent over coughing. When he straightened up, he continued to wipe at his eyes and his voice was hoarse. Now Axel could see that much of his clothing was burned or torn. There was only half of his new cloak, and what there was was missing the silver stars and moon. Axel noticed that even the white stains on the shoulders were gone or covered up with soot. And Cynthia was gone. He looked for Grrr and saw him almost at the woods, running hard in front of a black chicken.

Axel began to laugh and cough at the same time. Both men stood by the chimney and wiped their eyes and coughed and laughed for the next half hour or so. When they quieted down, they heard Winthton. The donkey had also run toward the woods and was standing on the edge of the depression coughing and shaking his head.

"This cavgon may need some refinements, Axel."

31

When the smoke and dust had blown away, Axel looked for the cavgon. He found the wheels on different sides of the chimney. The twisted frame was about a third of the way to the woods, and there was no sign of the barrel at all. That must have been what made the strange sounds like whistling that I heard just after the big boom, Axel thought. It must have been pieces of the iron wrapping flying in all directions.

Sidney sat at the foot of the chimney rock. He looked exhausted, and the fringe of white hair that circled his mostly bald head just above his ears was either gone or singed down to his scalp.

Axel sat next to him and said, "Too much firestarter powder?"

Sidney could see Axel's lips move but couldn't hear what he said. He frowned and Axel realized he could barely hear his own voice. The blast must have hurt Sidney's ears. He threw his hands into the air as he shouted, "Big ka-boom, eh?"

Sidney looked intently at Axel's lips as he spoke. When he saw them form the word *ka-boom* he laughed and said, "Big ka-boom."

The friends rested at the foot of the chimney rock until they could begin to hear each other speaking. Then Sidney stood and began to pound the soot out of his clothing. Axel helped by pounding him on the back. When Sidney felt he was as presentable as he was going to get, he said, "What do you think of research, Axel?"

"Which kind was that?"

Sidney smiled through the soot and said, "Wizards call that dynamic research. Not every wizard can do that kind. It takes nerve."

Axel looked for Grrr and saw him standing with Winthton. There was a dark ball by Winthton's feet, so Sidney's chicken must be all right.

Axel examined the hole that had been blasted in the dirt where the cavgon had been. He looked over at Sidney and said, "If we listed the things that we have to work with to solve our problem, Sidney. I think it'd be a bit shorter now."

"We can't be defeated by a misstep, Axel. We just have to start over."

"You can start over if you want to. I'm going to the castle to find Molly, and then she and I'll talk about what we can do to find Sid." Axel headed for Winthton who was watching the two men with huge and wild eyes.

The men had left their horses in the woods at the edge of the depression. They knew the cavgon would scare them and they wanted to save them that experience. Sidney had felt that Winthton wouldn't be bothered by the any loud noises.

"Wait for me, Axel. I'll go with you," Sidney said, using the tall stone to help him get upright. "There's nothing left for me to do here and I want to help."

When they reached Winthton, Grrr and Cynthia, Sidney put his chicken on his shoulder. At first she didn't want to have Sidney touch her and tried to avoid his hands, but once Sidney had put her on his shoulder, the well singed chicken dug her claws in, and with wide eyes, settled in for the trip home.

The ride back to Amory was a good deal quicker than the one out to the chimney rock. When they were on the crest of the last hill north of Willardville, the castle bell rang.

Axel stopped his horse and said, "Wait, Sidney."

When Sidney turned and looked at his friend, he saw that Axel had his hand up in a gesture that said wait. "What is it?"

"Just a bit ago I heard the bell ring."

"And?"

"But just one time?"

The bell rang again and Axel said, "There it is again. There must be a count of at least 30 between rings. What's that mean, Sidney?"

"Not good, Axel," Sidney said, and he looked at the castle. They could see it plainly, for the day had turned clear and the sun was setting on their right. The shadows of the trees that lined the west side of the roadway were long and dark as they lay across their path.

There were dark birds swirling in large groups that were massing for their flight south for the winter. They'd settle by the hundreds in the bare trees, and at some silent signal, would all rise at the same time and fly off as if they comprised one animal.

Axel watched them work together and was amazed at their cooperation. They seemed to know exactly when to turn and wheel, for the whole group would do it together. How much smarter they are than us, he thought. We have to have leaders to tell us who to hate and kill, and here are these dumb birds which can live and work without constantly fighting.

The bell rang again. When Axel looked back at the castle, the tall spires and the flags that flew from masts on their tops were shining in the setting sun. The rest of the buildings were in deep shadow and almost black.

"What do you mean when you say 'Not good'?"

"They only ring the bell that way when someone's died. I'd think that this time it's the king."

"King Willard's dead?"

"I don't know for sure, Your Highness."

Axel turned quickly and frowned at his friend, "What?"

"If that's for the king, you're king now, you know."

"That can't be right. There has to be more to this king business than that, doesn't there?"

Sidney looked at Axel as if he didn't understand why he would ask that question. "No, that's all there is to it."

The bell rang. "You're prince, the king dies, you're king. It's that simple, Axel."

"What if I don't want to be king?"

"There's no question there. You don't have a choice about it." Sidney studied Axel for a moment, but Axel was still looking at the castle and shaking his head.

The bell rang.

Sidney rode on saying, "Come on, Axel, we should be back before full dark."

32

Sid dumped a basket of charcoal into the forge's firebox. He had been at it most of the day and didn't remember when he'd been so tired. He didn't know whether it was harder pumping the bellows or carrying charcoal. Pump and carry. Pump and carry. He'd had chores on the farm, but there was never a hurry, and there was always something different to do. But here it was pump and carry and that's all.

He wiped his hand across his face to clear some of the charcoal dust from his eyes and eyebrows and thought about eating. Do people feed their apprentices? He put the basket he was carrying down next to a small pile of baskets and walked to the other side of the furnace and grabbed onto the two-handled bellows. He could feel the blisters forming on his palms.

The bellows were for pumping air into the bottom of the furnace under the burning charcoal. It had a long handle connected to a large leather bag. When he lifted it up, air was drawn into the bag, and when he pushed down, that air was forced out of the bag through a leather hose.

He pumped until the charcoal glowed and sent up sparks and he could feel the heat radiating from it. When it was as hot as he knew the blacksmith wanted it to be, he went to the back of the shop for more charcoal.

"Hey, Boy," the blacksmith yelled into the darkness.

Sid was filling a basket with the dusty charcoal and looked up and yelled, "What?"

"You hungry?"

"Sure I am."

The large man laughed and said, "Come up here then." Sid did and the man pointed toward one corner of the very busy courtyard. "See there? In the corner. That colored wagon? I think they're selling some kind of food. Here's a coin. You go over and get us both some and don't get run over by all the army boys." He laughed.

Sid didn't want to leave the darkness of the shop. He knew that the men still must be looking for him. A strange boy his age in the courtyard would be sure to attract attention. While he was thinking this, he was watching people line up at a window cut into the side of the wagon.

It had been drawn by an old sway-backed horse which was still hitched and standing patiently. The wagon was the most colorful thing Sid had ever seen. It was painted in red and white stripes. It was covered and the roof was white and black. The wheels were blue and the frame green. There was someone selling something out of a window cut in the center of the wagon.

The cutout section had been split. The upper half opened upward, forming an awning, and was propped up by sticks. The bottom half had been lowered and rested on poles. This served as a counter where the people put whatever it was they were selling.

Sid was trying to think of some way to avoid going into the courtyard when a large group of people around his own age ran through the big gate. He thought that they must have been working in the fields and were in for lunch or something. When they saw the wagon, they threaded their way through the crowds of men with weapons and lined up at the window. They must have been told to do this for they hadn't hesitated.

Now is a good time, Sid said to himself. Anyone seeing me will assume I'm one of them. He ran from the shop and joined the line at its end. Clutching the coin, he shuffled forward slowly as the line shortened.

Two men stopped and looked carefully at the line of children, and both heads stopped moving when they saw Sid. The rest of the children weren't clean, but they weren't black with charcoal dust and didn't have dirty rags tied around their mouths and noses, and it must have seemed strange to them that Sid did.

They watched Sid move slowly to the window. Sid tried not to show that he was aware that they were looking at him. When he was only three from the front of the line, they walked to where he was waiting and the taller of the two said, "How'd ya get so dirty, Boy? None a the others look like you."

Sid felt cold. Would he have to go back to that dark room in the basement? He didn't know what to say. He turned and looked back at the blacksmith shop. When he turned, the two men turned also, and just then the blacksmith waved his arm in a hurry up gesture. Sid held his hands out from his sides signalling that he had no choice. When he did, the men glanced at each other then walked away to look into other shops and dark corners.

Sid turned back toward the wagon and saw that the line was gone. He was alone in front of the window.

33

Axel reined in his horse just before they crossed the drawbridge and Sidney stopped with him. "Sidney," Axel said, "You have to help me out of this king thing."

The bell rang.

Sidney was surprised that Axel would say that right out by the entrance. What if someone heard him? He glanced around and fortunately they were alone. "You don't have a choice, Axel."

Axel smiled and said, "Sure I do. I just say 'No, thank you,' and we go back to the valley."

Sidney said, "Let's not talk about this here, Axel. We don't want anyone to overhear us." He reached up and petted Cynthia. His chicken was mostly naked except for the blackened stubs of feathers. Sidney had tied a bit of blue cloth around her to keep her warm.

They crossed the moat and turned in the courtyard toward the stable. After they had handed over their horses to a stableboy and given him instructions about feeding and brushing down Winthton, Axel said, "Come with me for a walk, Sidney. We have to talk."

The bell rang.

"Sure, where?"

"Somewhere away from the castle. I need to have you help me think about this problem."

The two friends walked back out the main entrance and turned to the side of the castle that faced the sea. They stepped over the broken rubble left from building the walls. The sun had set, but there were still no clouds and the moon was almost full and had risen, so it was light enough for them to see when they had reached the edge of the cliff.

A bright yellow stripe on top of the waves stretched all the way to the horizon just below the moon.

The bell rang.

Axel stood on the very edge and watched the waves crash and sparkle in the moonlight against the foundation of the castle. Even though this action was a good bit below them, it was easy to hear the pounding.

"Please help me, Sidney."

"Axel, I'd do anything for you I could. You should know that. But, I don't know what to do. You promised you'd be king. You can't say no now."

"Why not?"

Sidney placed his hands on Axel's shoulders and, looking into his face, he said, "You've promised the king and that means that you promised all the people in the kingdom."

The bell rang.

"I don't want to be king. I don't think Molly wants to be queen. I know neither of us wants to leave the valley and live here. And besides all that, I don't want Sid to be the next king when I die. I think he'd be happier being a farmer."

Sidney dropped his hands and shook his head. "You're needed, Axel."

"By who? And why?"

"You're needed by the people who trust you." He swept his arm out to include the castle and the town of Willardville. "Not just anybody can be a leader. Only special people. When one of these special people is called on to serve the rest of us, they have to do what they can. This isn't something that's easy, but then the good things never are, Axel."

"I wasn't born to be a king. I'm just a farmer who wants to be left alone."

The bell rang.

"That can't be helped now. All people have to have someone in their lives they can look up to. We all need to feel protected by someone. We need to know that when we need help there will be someone who'll help us. At this time that someone for these people is you. You don't have a choice about this."

Axel watched the waves pound the huge stones. The spray was cold against his face and the air blowing from the sea, up and over the edge, smelled of salt and fish.

Axel lifted his eyes and followed the yellow line to the moon and saw his valley and Molly and Sid and himself sitting on the edge of the well, waiting in the evenings for deer to pick their way down from the hills to eat in the meadow and drink at the lake. They were dainty and always looked as though they expected trouble.

The many deer became one doe which stood in the darker edge of the trees and watched the clearing for long enough to be sure it was safe. Very slowly she stepped from the trees and waited, her head held up and still, watching and scenting.

When she knew the valley was clear, she walked to the water, and as she drank, lifted her head and gazed bright-eyed, a new direction each time. In the spring there would be fawns with their soft white spots that looked like the flowers that dotted the meadow. At some signal, two fawns would pick their way to her and nudge her underside with their noses. They would have trouble concentrating on why they were there; they'd nurse while their mother nibbled the thick grasses, then run off on legs large-jointed and awkward. He heard Molly's soft laughter and Sid's bright, quick questions.

The bell rang.

"That's a lot of responsibility you're giving me, Sidney."

Sidney was quite for a moment, then said, "No, Axel, I'm not giving it to you. A person can't give something like that. Responsibility is something that each of us has to recognize for ourselves. If I had to give it to you, you wouldn't be ready for it and would fail to meet it. When you can see it for yourself, that's when you know you can accept it as yours."

"What if I don't see this as my responsibility now?"

The bell rang.

"Then you won't stay here and be king."

"It's as easy as that?"

Sidney shook his head. "That's not easy, Axel. To refuse responsibility is sometimes a lot harder than it is to accept it."

Axel turned and faced his friend and asked, "Why is that?"

"Because of the consequences."

"What's that mean?"

Sidney shook his head when he said, "Maybe you're not ready after all, Axel. What will happen is that Rohn will be king. You'll have given him the kingdom. What do you think that'll mean for everyone else? You have to decide if he'll be a good king for us."

"Us?"

"Sure, you live here in the kingdom too, you know. So do Molly and Sid."

The bell rang.

Axel turned and looked at the castle. His eyes followed the tallest tower to its top where the bell hung. He looked at the dark and shadowed belfry and thought about what Sidney had said. The bell rang, and as the sound died away, he turned to his friend and said, "Sidney, I guess the bell is ringing for me."

34

Molly was more disappointed than she thought she ever could be, and so tired. She had hoped that she'd have a chance to talk to someone who would be able to tell her if they'd seen her son, but she'd had no chance to talk to anyone.

It had all depended on people liking her dragon ears. And that had been the trouble. Everyone loved them. She'd been busy all day making the dumb things and had had no time at all to ask anyone anything. Fry, roll, cut, pour, collect money, and start over again and again and again. It was dark and she hadn't asked about Sid at all.

She'd seen lots of children about his age but not him. There'd even been one little boy who hadn't looked at her but had held up two fingers to show that he wanted two dragon ears. She thought that he looked as if he wanted his mother. She could tell that was what he was thinking, even though all she could see of his face were white circles around his eyes, for the rest was covered with a dirty rag. That must be to keep the charcoal dust out of his lungs, she thought.

That really hurt her heart, and all the rest of him was covered with black. He must have been helping collect or make it. She thought that his hands had Sid's slender fingers and she had wanted to reach out and touch one. But she couldn't do it.

And just when she had started to speak to him as she handed him the dragon ears, he ran away as if he were scared or something. Sid would have spoken to her even if he were scared. And he must be, she thought. Her baby alone, and kept in some room with strangers. Not knowing where he was or what was going on or where his mother was. He didn't know that his parents were looking for him. No, he must know they would be.

Molly stood in the window of the gaily painted wagon and cried like she'd never cried before. Not just tears and sobs, but she emptied herself and could feel herself begin to turn inside out. All the fear, anxiety, and waiting poured out of her so that she was overwhelmed with feelings of loss and despair.

When she couldn't cry any longer, when she was dry and totally empty, when she could finally stand upright and face the world again, her legs were so weak that she had to sit on the short stool by the window. She sat there with her arms resting on the shelf and her head on her arms, and, looking across the courtyard, watched people going back to work after lunch.

Directly across from her wagon was a booth where someone was making baskets. That woman had a child, she thought, and she knew where he was. Next to that was a shop with a loom in the entrance. A woman was weaving a brightly colored blanket. Her child would be at home or working in the fields, or maybe even in the back of her shop.

And there was the blacksmith shop. She could see the large blacksmith pounding on something with a hammer and even hear the sound of it hitting the metal half a beat after she saw it bounce on the anvil, and the boy carrying a basket of charcoal he dumped into the fire. The sparks flew. The man said something to him and the boy hopped to the other side of the forge, and she could see him pumping on the handle of the largest bellows she had ever seen.

The boy was about Sid's age and about his size. Much too small to be working so hard. He had to jump onto a box to stretch his little arms up high enough to work the handle and then jump off and put his weight on the handle to force it down. His mother knew where he was, even if he was working so hard.

Molly wondered about his parents. Why would people give such a wonderful boy to a blacksmith? He should be at home with his mother.

She wished now that she had spoken to him as soon as she had seen him. Maybe tomorrow, if he comes again, he'll speak. Today the boy had held up just two fingers and pushed a coin across the counter, and all the while he was looking around as if he were afraid or was searching for someone. If he comes tomorrow, I'll tell him that I have a boy just like him. Maybe I'll have a chance to ask him if he's seen a strange boy here. I can hope.

Molly lowered the top half of the window and locked it in place, then brought up the bottom half and locked that. She was about to step out of the door and climb into the seat and drive back to the Gypsy camp when she noticed two dragon ears that she hadn't sold. She thought that the boy would like them. I'll just take them across the courtyard and hand them to him and walk away. I might even be able to get the blacksmith in a conver-sation. I could learn something today, after all.

35

Axel and Sidney didn't talk for some time. They both were well into their own thoughts. Axel couldn't stop thinking about what they could to do to find Sid. He felt that Molly must have taken the Gypsy wagon and gone to Rohn's castle. He didn't know what he could do about that. He couldn't go and get her. They might recognize him and that would give his family even more trouble.

Maybe she'd even come up with something. It would be so much better if only they knew where Sid was. Even knowing that he was all right would be better than this, not knowing anything.

Turning to his friend, Axel said, "Let's sit and talk about what we can do," and, without waiting for Sidney to reply, he sat with his legs hanging over the edge of the cliff. Grrr sat next to him and watched the water for any danger. Sidney sat on his other side and they watched the moon rise. Neither felt the need to speak, almost as if they had agreed not to talk until they had something important to contribute.

Axel asked, "Is there anything we can do until we find out what Molly's learned?"

Sidney didn't answer.

The bell rang.

"Sidney?"

"I'm thinking."

"Doing some of that research, are you?"

"You asked me to help, Axel. I'm trying."

Again Axel felt foolish for being impatient with his friend. He knew Sidney was trying because he cared for Sid, too.

"Sorry, Sidney."

The men sat silently.

The moon rose.

The bell rang.

Sidney shifted his weight on the stones of the cliff.

"You think of something?" Axel asked.

"Nothing you'd agree to."

"What?"

"It's got to do with killing, and I know you wouldn't put up with that."

Axel waited but Sidney didn't say any more. He couldn't stand it. "What did you think might work?"

Sidney filled his lungs and let the air out slowly before he said, "We could have lots of the new bows made, and, when Rohn found out that we could kill his knights easily, he might give up trying to take the kingdom."

"That doesn't sound like killing. We wouldn't have to kill the knights, just show that we could."

The bell rang.

We might have to kill one or two to convince him that we could. He wouldn't believe us if we just told him."

"A demonstration?"

"Just a knight or two, not many."

"Just kill one or two men? There must be a way to show him what the bow could do without shooting men with it."

"Shoot a tree?"

"Trees don't wear armor," Axel said.

Sidney jumped up and started walking around in small circles.

Axel turned and watched this over his shoulder for a while, then he said, "What is it? What did you think of?"

"I'm thinking, Axel."

"What?"

"Not done yet."

"Think out loud," Axel said, as he, too, stood and circled next to Sidney, watching his face intently.

The bell rang.

Sidney stopped walking, faced Axel and said, "We have a very strong bow."

Axel kept count, "One."

"We need Rohn to know that we can kill his knights with it any time we want to."

"Two."

"You don't want to kill anyone."

"Three."

"We'd do anything to get Sid back, including killing a knight or two."

Axel didn't answer. Here was the main problem again. He couldn't kill but he had to rescue his son. Two values in conflict. What does a person do when he can't keep both values intact, but he has to act?

The bell rang.

It felt to Axel like his mind was split into two pieces. One piece said that nothing was more important to him than getting Sid back. The other piece said that if he had values and broke some, the ones he ended up with wouldn't be worth anything. Was there some way to do what he had to do and not choose between them?

Axel said, "I can't go along with killing innocent men to demonstrate the power of a weapon, Sidney."

"What if that's the only thing we can think of?"

"Then we haven't thought hard enough."

"You wouldn't throw Sid away because you can't kill two knights, would you?"

"No. I couldn't throw Sid away for any reason."

Sidney held his arms out and said, "That settles it, then. We do what we have to do to get Sid back. It's that simple."

"Good. But we have to think of ways to do it without killing."

Sidney was losing patience with his friend. How could he be so stubborn? For Sidney, the answer was simple. Do what worked, whatever it was, and satisfy the major goal of rescuing Sid.

"Axel, you've got to give on this killing thing. Sid's your son. That has to be the most important thing in the world to you. Let's get the carpenters working on making the bows. It'll take some time because we'll need a bunch of them, so we'd better have them start in the morning."

The bell rang.

Axel pushed that idea away from him with his palms and said, "We should destroy that bow you have and forget all about it. That's a terrible weapon, and I don't want to have anything to do with it."

Sidney had had enough. "All right, Axel. Do what you want. I'm going to bed. Coming?" Sidney was already moving toward the castle.

"No, you go on. I've got some thinking to do and I might as well do it here as anywhere."

Axel watched as Sidney walked away and disappeared in the shadows of the castle's high walls.

36

When Sid had first seen his mother, he'd had trouble believing it was really her. How could it be? In this strange place, selling bread out of a Gypsy wagon? He knew that's what it was because there'd been a camp of them outside Greenwater when his parents had taken him to visit. This wagon looked just like those had.

It was hard for Sid to not yell out when he'd recognized his mother. He'd wanted to climb right over the counter and grab onto her and have her hold him, but he couldn't do that. He didn't know whose castle they were in, but he knew they weren't in a friendly one or they wouldn't be here. If his mother was in a Gypsy wagon selling bread, no telling what was going on.

Maybe she was in trouble, too. If he said anything to her, it might make things worse. If she were still here tomorrow, maybe he'd have a chance to talk to her. Maybe she didn't recognize him. He sure didn't look like he had the last time she'd seen him. All covered with charcoal dust and with a dirty rag covering half his face. Now he wasn't sure she'd have known him even if he'd said something to her.

Sid was sure that the men were still looking for him. They must have wanted him for something important to kidnap him right in front of his house. It was a lot of trouble bringing him to this castle, wherever it was, and putting him in a small room like that.

If he talked to his mother tomorrow, he'd have to be sure the men who were looking for him weren't around. He sure didn't want to get his mother in trouble.

Sid returned to the blacksmith shop and the blacksmith gave him one of the dragon ears. Sid recognized the taste and it made him homesick.

Sid could tell when it was evening for it was much darker in the shop. He was in the back filling baskets with charcoal from a large pile, getting ready for work in the morning. He had to bank the fire. The blacksmith had explained how to do it, and he thought he understood.

Sid heard his mother's voice. She was talking to the blacksmith about dragon ears. He tossed the basket down and started toward the front of the shop.

"I had two left and I thought you and your boy would like them. Better than throwing them away."

"What ya want for 'em?"

"Nothing. I'll leave them for you and the boy."

Sid could see her now at the entrance, but he was sure she couldn't see him. It was dark in the back.

"Give 'em to me?"

"You and the boy."

Sid could see her hand the ears to the blacksmith. "I noticed that the boy bought two earlier today."

"What you care about the boy?" There was a sound of suspicion in his voice. "Not yours is he?"

Sid didn't dare go to the front of the shop. He didn't trust the blacksmith yet, and he didn't know what he'd do if he learned who he was. Probably call the guards.

"Oh, no. I didn't recognize him. But he's like a boy I knew once. Molly wiped some honey off her hand on the cloth and said, "I'll have more tomorrow and if you send the boy over, I'll be sure to sell him hot ones."
That settled it. His mother didn't want anyone to know who she was. He couldn't give her away, either. He'd have to be extra careful tomorrow.

37

Axel had never felt so alone. Even when he was trapped in the dragon's cave, underground, with the dragon sitting on the entrance, he hadn't felt so cut off. Now his wife was gone off with Gypsies, his son kidnapped by strangers, his king blind, deaf and dying, maybe even dead, and his only long-time friend didn't understand how strongly he felt about not killing anything ever again.

The wind had gained strength and was throwing the spray from the waves up to the top of the cliff, and there the droplets were freezing on whatever they hit. He wiped his face with his hand and there was more water on it than would be caused by the spray. Axel realized he was crying in frustration and disappointment.

He understood that he didn't make the world he was in, and his situation was not because of things he'd done, but a man is supposed to be able to take care of his family. Axel felt that somehow he was failing. This might not be a reasonable way to think, but that didn't matter, that's what he felt.

He sat on the cliff's edge and watched the moon rise to a thin line of clouds and disappear briefly behind them. He had to do something to help his son. Sid and Molly were the most important people in his world, and he couldn't help them. It wasn't fair. He didn't deserve this. Other people never had these terrible things happen to them. The sobs racked his shoulders, the tears ran down his face, his chest convulsed with the pain of the tension and its release.

He cried for a few minutes, and felt somewhat better. Axel said to himself, I can't sit here feeling sorry for myself, looking at the moon and crying. Good people don't give up. They have things they love, they have principles they fight for, they have values that guide their lives and I've got them, too. I can be as strong as any trouble I run into. I don't have to give up. I don't have Sidney here to help me think, but I can think on my own, and, maybe I can use his system to solve this problem.

He held mental fingers up as he thought of points. I've got a problem I can't run away from and it has to be solved soon. The Molly part of the problem can wait, though. I don't know where she is, but I don't know that she's in trouble, either. She may be all right, and she might even be finding out things that we need to know.

The king business. The king dying and me being made king doesn't have to be solved right away. I can put that part of the whole problem off for a while and look at it later.

Rohn wanting to be king is natural. He's the king's younger brother. It doesn't matter if he's not a good man, he's still in line for the throne. The king adopting me just complicates things. I don't have to do anything about that until the king dies. That may not be what the bell was for. Don't worry about it now.

The Sid part of the problem, the most important part, is the one I have to work on. But, I can't do anything about that till I know where he is. Molly's working on that part. I have to hope that Molly can find out something, wherever she is.

The last part of the problem is what to do about the possibility of Rohn attacking Amory and Willardville. I'm a knight. I accepted the honor and did enjoy the idea for years. I'm a prince, even if it doesn't make any sense, it's still the way it is. So, I do have responsibilities to the king, the people in the castle and the people in town. I can't turn my back on this part of the problem. When I accepted the honor, I also accepted the duty. I can work on this part of the problem now.

Axel was beginning to feel better. He felt that his thinking was clearer. He was making decisions that made sense. Also, he thought that, before he could make a plan, he had to list the things he could do and what he couldn't do and what he had to work with. Sidney had taught him that, and it had worked for him in the past.

"What I have to work with I should list first," he said out loud. "One, I have Sidney and his crazy mind. Two, I have his research projects. Three, I can use anything in the castle to help. Four, I have the king's knights and army to help me if I need them. The king will support me in this if I need him to. . . .If he's alive.

"Now for what I can't do. One, I can't expect the problem to go away by itself. Two, I can't not try and solve the problem. Three, I can't do anything that involves killing anyone. Four, I can't do anything that puts Sid or Molly in more danger than they're in already."

Axel realized that he was shivering and when he wiped his face he could feel the ice in his hair. He reached over and ran his hand down Grrr's back and there was ice in his fur. "We've got to go back inside and get warm. I can't do anyone any good if I'm frozen."

He felt that his time had been well spent. He didn't know more now than he had, but he was making decisions and was about to make a plan. But, that could wait until he was sitting next to the stove in the kitchen.

38

The heat felt good. The old cook wasn't there, but Axel found bread and some milk that was still fresh. There was a large bone on the cutting board with a good bit of meat still clinging to it. The bone was much too heavy for his dog to manage, but when he held it down, Grrr was eager to take it and was careful where he put his teeth. Grrr took a grip on the bone and pulled, and, when Axel let go, his end of the bone hit the stone floor, and this caused Grrr to let go of his end. As soon as Grrr had another firm grip on the large bone, he dragged it near the stove, lay down and began to pull at the meat.

This was a much more comfortable place to plan than sitting on the edge of the cliff in the freezing salt spray. Axel actually felt good. The food and being warm were part of it, but the idea that he was making some progress with his problem was the real reason.

He felt decisive. He had to stop Rohn's men and at the same time not kill them. That sounded simple enough. Let's see, how to go about it? Talk them into peace? That was silly, but he had to think of everything, no matter how dumb it sounded. Sometimes the dumb things were the ones that worked.

All right. If he couldn't talk to them, at least he could demonstrate the power of the bow to them. How could he do that without talking? There's a nice problem. Show someone something without telling them what they're seeing. Is it even possible? And if it is, would it work? If Rohn knew about the bow, would that stop him sending his knights to attack the castle?

Axel saw a row of King Willard's archers lining both sides of the road. Rohn's knights on horseback charging four abreast and all the archers firing at the same time and the first row of knights falling backward off their horses. The first row of archers replaced by another row of men with armed bows and the second row of knights charging over their dead comrades and then being hit by the second flight of arrows. The second row of knights falling like the first. The second row of archers being replaced by—

What Axel had to do was get Rohn to see the same scene in his mind. Axel was sure that if Rohn ever had a chance he'd kill him instantly, so, he had to do this without talking to him. This meant that he had to show him what it would mean to attack the king's castle.

Once Rohn understood that King Willard could kill his knights any time they charged against his archers, he wouldn't chance an attack. Axel felt it was now time to ask Sidney for help. He had a plan, and what he had to do was to figure out how to get it to work.

Axel was stepping out of the kitchen when he stopped and looked back at Grrr. The dog was standing with one end of the large bone in his mouth. He could drag it, but it left a heavy grease smear on the floor. Moving with it was a job even for so big a dog, and very messy.

Feeling the need to be close to someone, and there being no one else there, Axel sat in the almost black corner with his hand on his dog's back as Grrr ate. Grrr didn't understand what was happening. He glanced at Axel, then at his bone. He might have thought that Axel wanted some and he wasn't eager to share. When Axel didn't make any move on the wonderful bone, Grrr again concentrated on his meal.

Axel heard footsteps in the hall and through the entrance to the dark kitchen stepped Sidney. He was talking and Axel assumed he had someone with him, but, when no one else came through the doorway, Axel realized that Sidney was alone. But who was he talking to? He wasn't mumbling like he usually did when he talked to himself. He was speaking right out loud. Axel was about to say something to his friend when Sidney, having picked up a cup from the edge of the sink and filled it with water, sat at the table and continued to talk.

"All this talk about principles when things have to be done they just get in the way always have and always will for people who think about things too much spend all their time thinking and not doing what has to be done so it's people like me who have to do the important stuff but I know he's got a problem with his family and so what I've got is problems with the whole kingdom and I'm not sitting around brooding about what I can't do, I'm working on solving problems all the time."

Axel didn't like the idea that he was listening to his friend when his friend didn't know he was there, but by this time it was too late. It was so dark in the corner where he and the dog sat that he knew Sidney hadn't seen them. Sidney was quiet for a while, and Axel was just about to stand and say something when Sidney started talking again.

"We can kill Rohn's knights but no we can't kill anyone so how are we going to convince Rohn to stop trying to take over the kingdom we don't know but let's sit down and think about it."

Sidney tipped the last of the water into his mouth and banged the cup on the table. He was still talking as he left the room.

Axel felt ashamed that he'd heard his friend talking about him. He hadn't realized that Sidney felt so strongly about his desire not to kill. If the wizard had been with me when I killed those dragons, he'd feel just the same way I do, he thought.

I guess I'll have to work on these problems without his help. That'll make it harder, but if I ask him to help me, I know he'll do it because he's my friend, but now I know his heart won't be in it. He'll do it for me, but not because he wants to. He'll feel he has to and I don't want to put him in that position.

There, I have another problem on top of all the rest of them. How to deal with Sidney and not let him know I know how he really feels without letting him know how I know it.

I can deal with that later. Now I have to figure out how to let Rohn know about the bow and what it can do. What he needs is a demonstration, but I have to give him one that doesn't kill one of his knights.

I have to let someone from his castle watch me shooting an arrow through armor. If he doesn't know that I know that he's watching, he'll still know that we really can do it. Rohn'll think about it and call off any plans to take over the kingdom.

Axel thought about the time when he was practicing with his bow and King Willard's man was watching him. That man told the king and the knights tried shooting arrows at a dragon and the dragon killed some of them. A little bit of knowing something sometimes is worse than a lot of ignorance. Could that be true? Is it better not to know? What about the saying, "What you don't know, won't hurt you." Is that true?

Axel realized he was thinking about dumb stuff because he didn't know what to do. Concentrate.

He had to get Sidney's bow, put it on a stand or have Sidney make it lighter and let Rohn's men see him practicing with it. This was fine, but what if they took it away from him. Then Rohn's archers would have it and King Willard's wouldn't.

I have to practice where I can be seen but nobody can get the bow away from me. Where they can see the arrows go through the armor or see that they have. What I need is a spy for Rohn. There might even be one right here in the castle. I need Sidney now.

Axel called to Grrr and the dog left his bone, but he didn't want to. He looked back at it all the while he was leaving the kitchen. They hurried to Sidney's room. Axel pounded on the door and Sidney opened it almost immediately.

"Axel," Sidney said, swinging the door fully open. "Come on in. I was just thinking about you and our problem."

Axel stepped into the small room.

39

The blacksmith let Sid sleep in a pile of hay in a corner of the shop. His muscles ached from the work that he wasn't used to and this pile of hay was more comfortable than the one in the room he had been in last night. He missed his mother and father and Rotug and Grrr and the cow and the chickens and the lake and fishing and. . . .

In the morning before full light, two guards talking in the courtyard woke Sid. He couldn't hear any other people moving yet but he couldn't go back to sleep. He washed his hands and face in the bucket that stood by the forge. I should fill it with fresh water, he thought. There was a well in the courtyard that most of the people who worked in the shops used and Sid filled the bucket there.

Iron bars had to be raised to open the big doors to the courtyard, and when Sid heard the chain rattle in the wheel, he turned to watch as the gates rose to the top of the arch. The thick wooden door then swung down to make a bridge over the moat. It was lowered on another chain that was wound on different wheel. The wheels had spokes men could grasp and there were catches that kept the wheels from spinning freely.

Sid walked closer to look at the machinery. He was standing at the entrance watching the men work when the bridge dropped into place. He glanced out the door and there was the same Gypsy wagon he'd seen yesterday waiting to enter. . .and his mother.

Sid hadn't tied the cloth over his face yet and had cleaned off some of the black, so he knew his mother would recognize him if she saw him clearly. He moved to the side of the entrance where she had to see him and looked upward toward the wagon.

Molly was surprised to see the boy she had given the dragon ears to yesterday standing by the gate. He didn't have the rag over his face and he wasn't covered in so much charcoal dust, but even in this dim light she could see that his clothes and hair were the same.

The guard was waving for her to hurry through the gate and she slapped the reins against the horse's back and the wagon moved into the courtyard. Sid slid the cloth from his neck and over his face.

When she was just above the boy, she looked down at him again. This time his face was covered, but he winked at her. She couldn't be mistaken. He had winked. What could that mean? He knew her? He certainly would recognize her from yesterday because she had given him free dragon ears, but a wink?

Sid had covered his face just before the wagon moved forward because he didn't want his mother to say anything when she recognized him. He wanted her to know that this boy was hers, but he didn't want it to happen at the gate where the guard was standing. He couldn't let anyone know who he was, and he was afraid if she recognized him, she'd jump off the wagon and hug him or something. He wanted her to hug him more than he had ever wanted anything, but he had to be careful. How to tell her that there was danger? He'd winked.

Sid felt that his mother would think it was strange to have a dirty, strange boy wink at her. But maybe she'd think about it during the day, and if the blacksmith sent him over to the wagon to buy dragon ears later, she might ask him why he'd winked and somehow he could let her know who he was.

Sidney's room was the same as most of the rooms in the castle. It had a narrow bed with a straw-filled mattress, a small table with a stool, a lamp and one very thin window. Axel knew that the windows were thin so that archers could shoot out of them and be well protected. And they let less winter wind in.

"What's the news, Axel? Have you heard from Molly?" Sidney asked.

"No. I need your thinking on something. Can we sit and talk for a bit?"

Sidney motioned toward the chair and sat on the bed. When Axel was seated, Sidney said, "You know I'll do what I can even if it means that I'll have to think."

Axel leaned forward and put his elbows on his knees and asked, "Does Rohn have a spy in the castle?"

Sidney didn't move or answer, he just looked at Axel. When he did speak, he used a very soft voice. "What have you been up to, Axel?"

"Nothing. I need to know about a spy."

"Why?"

"No, spy."

"No spy?"

"Yes spy."

"Why spy?"

Axel felt better now that he and Sidney could kid again. He had been wrong to feel badly about his old friend. "I want to be sure Rohn learns about your new lighter bow. The one that our archers can hold in their hands and shoot like a regular bow."

"I didn't know I had a lighter bow."

"Sure, you do. You and I are going to make it tonight."

Sidney stretched out on the bed and said, "I was just about to go to sleep, Axel."

Standing up, Axel said, "Come on, Sidney, we've got work to do. We can sleep later."

Sidney sat up and said, "Before I do anything, you've got to tell me what you have in mind."

Axel explained to his friend what he had imagined about the king's archers shooting Rohn's knights. When he explained that they could do the same thing without killing anyone and how they could do it, Sidney jumped up and danced about the room with his strange hopping dance. He slapped his hands against his legs. He brought his knees up, one at a time and jumped with the other leg and all the time he bobbed his head. He was laughing and saying, "Yes, yes, yes."

Grrr followed him about the room. It looked to Axel as if the dog were trying either to imitate Sidney or to dance with him.

Sid had the fire hot by the time the blacksmith walked into his shop. He didn't greet Sid or say anything except, "Eat yet?"

Sid said he hadn't and the blacksmith handed him some bread and cheese that was wrapped in a cloth. Sid sat and ate after filling a cup with water.

When the blacksmith examined the forge he nodded and Sid could hear him mumble to himself. He turned and looked out of the front of the shop for a moment and turned to Sid and said, "That Gypsy's here again selling them dragon ears. You want one?"

Sid had his mouth full of bread and had just bitten into the cheese and couldn't speak, but he nodded his head. The blacksmith dug into his apron and put a coin on the edge of the anvil and said, "When you're done eating, you go and get two. I like 'em myself."

Sid could feel his heart pounding and his mouth got so dry he had to drink to swallow the cheese.

He held the coin tightly in his hand as he crossed the courtyard. It was early and there were only two other people moving that he could see. The window in the wagon hadn't been opened yet, but his mother was putting a bucket of water down for the horse to drink. Sid waited until he was sure no one was watching, and stood by the window.

When Molly turned back toward the wagon, there was that boy who had winked at her. She didn't know why but she felt drawn to him. He didn't have the cloth over his face now but he was in dark shadow by the side of the wagon and she couldn't see him clearly.

"Up early, are we?" Molly asked as she walked toward this strange boy.

Sid said in a very low voice so that no one else would hear, "I usually get up early, Mother."

Molly stopped herself from yelling out just in time. The cry was in her throat and just behind her tongue when she put her hands to her mouth to hold it in.

She tried not to, but she hurried to her son with her hands out. Sid shook his head and said in an even lower voice, "They can't know you're my mother. They're looking for me. They kept me in a small room but I got away and now I'm working for the blacksmith."

Molly couldn't stop herself from touching Sid. She put her hand on his cheek and it felt wonderful. "Get in the wagon, Sid and we'll leave now."

Shaking his head, Sid said, "We can't do that. The blacksmith knows I came here, and you just got here and it'd look funny if you left right away. We have to wait till tonight and then I'll hide in the wagon and no one'll miss me and they'll expect you to leave, anyway. The black-smith sent me over for two dragon ears. He gave me this coin." Sid handed it to his mother.

"I've got some that are still warm. I made them just before I came in the gate." She stepped into the wagon and the top half of the window opened, then the bottom half dropped down and there they were, mother and son, doing business.

42

Sidney had to light a lamp before they could see anything at all in the small room where he worked on his research. When it was lighted and the door was locked, he said, "You said I had a lighter bow. Tell me about that."

Axel loosened the clamps that held Sidney's experimental bow onto the workbench and picked it up. It was heavy. He examined it from all angles. When he put it back on the bench, he pointed to it and said, "Show me what parts of it can be made smaller, thinner or shorter."

Sidney picked it up and he turned it over and over. Axel could hear him mumble softly to himself, "Yes here and. . .some here. . .uh-huh. . .yes and here." He looked at Axel and said, "I don't think I can, Axel."

"But. . .I heard you just now. . . . Of course, you can, Sidney. You have to."

The old wizard held up his hands in front of his face. The fingers looked more twisted and bent than Axel remembered from the last time he had seen them. "They aren't any better now than they were when you wanted me to make that bow for you," Sidney said.

Now Axel understood. Sidney wanted him to do the work. Well, that was fine, he'd be glad to. He knew that Sidney would be sitting on a stool telling him just what to do.

"I can do the work. If you'll tell me what to do, we should be able to get this done tonight."

"I think tomorrow would be a good time to start this project. I was just going to bed when you knocked on my door. I may be too sleepy to do a good job."

"We don't have a choice. Too much depends on us making sure Rohn learns about this bow. Remember, Sid

163

and Molly are out there somewhere. We have to do this as quickly as we can, so we have to start now."

Sidney nodded his head and said, "You're right, Axel. Tonight it is."

The two friends worked most of the night. The bow they ended up with didn't look much like the one Sidney had first showed to Axel. It was much shorter, for Sidney hadn't thought that the first version might be held by an archer and had a long piece of wood for a frame that would have to be set on a wagon.

The trigger mechanism was smoother, and the part that held the arrow was almost half as thick as it had been. They had talked about each piece of the bow and what it did, and only then figured out how light it could be and still do the job.

When the new bow was finished, Axel fired it at the door. He was surprised that there wasn't the bang that he'd heard with the other one. Of course, there was a jerk when the trigger was pulled and the bow straightened pulling the arrow forward, but there was almost no sound. Just the bow string vibrating and the sound of the arrow going through the door.

They opened the door and examined the two arrows sticking out of the wood. Both shafts had penetrated about the same distance, and they couldn't tell which one had been fired first.

"That was a good night of research, Axel," Sidney said, feeling the points of the arrows.

"If I remember right, research means that we knew what we were doing and how to go about doing it. Is that right?"

"You got it, my boy."

"Now we have to find some armor for the demon-stration," Axel said.

"Can't we just shoot it through a piece of wood? The spy should understand what it can do."

Axel frowned and said, "What spy?"

"You said you needed one."

Turning his friend to face him, Axel said, "You thought of a spy? Good for you, Sidney. I knew I could count on you for help. Who is it?"

Sidney sat on the bed and said, "It doesn't matter who it is, any spy will do."

"What's that mean?"

"You care who the spy is?"

This was confusing Axel. Did Sidney have a spy or not? "I don't care who it is as long as we know he's a spy."

Sidney gestured toward the chair and said, "Here's the problem we got. We need a spy to tell Rohn about the bow, right?"

Axel sat and nodded, "Right."

"We don't know his name, right?"

"But you said—"

"I didn't say I knew who the spy was, just that I had one."

"How could you have one and not know who it is?"

Sidney held his hands out to the sides of his body and, tilting his head to the left said, "There has to be one in the castle somewhere. What goes on here is known about right away at Rohn's castle. We get reports from there that they know what we're doing and talking about. So, we got a spy, we just don't know his name."

"That makes sense now that you explain it."

Taking the bow and three arrows that were lying on the bench, Sidney headed out of the room. Axel stopped him by grabbing onto his arm.

"Where are you going?"

"To the kitchen."

"Why."

"To let the spy know that we're going to demonstrate the bow."

"Axel held onto the arm and said, "I don't understand and I should."

"If we sit in the kitchen and put the bow on the table, everyone who comes in will see it. They'll ask about it and when they do, we'll tell them we're going to test it in the courtyard just before noon."

Axel nodded his head then turned it to the side and stood still.

"What's the matter, Axel?"

"I don't hear the bell."

Sidney listened a moment then said, "I don't either. They must have stopped ringing it. We should see what it was about. Let's go up and see what's going on in the hallway outside the king's rooms."

Axel held up his hand and shaking his head said, "The first thing we have to do is set up the demonstration so we'll be sure the spy will hear of it by noon. If the king is really dead, two hours won't make any difference, and if he's not dead, it won't matter whether we go up there or not."

Sidney could see the logic of that, and he picked up the bow and they headed for the kitchen.

43

Sid watched what was going on at the wagon whenever he had a chance to be near the front of the shop. But the blacksmith kept him busy, for he had a special commission from Rohn, making armor and arms. Sid felt the urgency as men came to the shop to be fitted or to order things to be made.

There was a line at the Gypsy wagon most of the day. The people in Rohn's castle liked the dragon ears and Molly made and sold them as fast as she could. She thought that she'd have to tell her father about this experience, and if he called what he made dragon ears, he might be able to make money from them, too.

The blacksmith sent Sid back at noon to buy two more. Again there was a long line and Sid had to stand in it. He kept the cloth over his face, and since he had no change of clothes, the ones he wore were almost black with charcoal dust.

The two men were still examining all the children they saw, but remembered Sid from yesterday and that he worked for the blacksmith. They ignored him.

Standing in line, Sid had a chance to look about. It was then that he realized that the gate was being guarded. There were three guards that were questioning everyone who wanted to leave the castle. They must be looking for me, he thought. He and his mother would have to be careful when they left.

The woman in front of Sid paid for her ears and turned away from the wagon, and there he was, facing his mother again. This time she knew who the boy under all the charcoal dust was, and it was all she could do to keep from crawling over the shelf and grabbing and holding him.

Sid put the coin on the shelf and said, "Two dragon ears, please."

Molly glanced at the person behind her son, saw that he wasn't paying any attention to them, and said, "How many and. . .when." She accentuated the *when* by pausing just before she said it.

Sid noticed the pause and thought it strange. That's no way for a person to talk who wants to sell something— she must be giving me a message. The part that didn't fit was the word, *when*. The whole sentence was a question, so she must be asking me to tell her when. When what?

"Two, please."

"And when?"

There it is again. *when*. . .She wants to know when something's going to happen. My mother either thinks I already know or she wants me to decide when something was.

Sid didn't know what to say. He looked into his mother's eyes. He saw worry. He saw love. He saw fear. What he didn't see was *when*.

Molly must have known that her son was confused by the looks he was giving her. The question seemed simple to her. Here he was, an escaped ransom victim, hiding out in a blacksmith shop, a way of getting safely away presents itself, all he has to do is tell her when he'll be able to sneak into the wagon and hide so she can drive the wagon out the gate and away, and he looks like he can't understand what she wants.

Molly put one dragon ear on the counter and smiled at her son. The man behind Sid was getting impatient and was watching what was going on. When Sid didn't take the ear, Molly said, "Here is the one you ordered for now. When do you want to come back for the other one?"

There, that ought to do it. He's a smart boy and he sure can figure that one out.

Sid understood. His mother wanted to know when he could be back. She must want to sneak him out of the castle today.

They had to be careful here. Everything had to look normal to the men searching for him. The blacksmith quit work when it was first dark. That would be a good time for a Gipsy wagon to leave the castle, too.

"Just as it gets dark, please."

"That's fine. I'll be looking for you," Molly said and smiled. She looked away from her son's face and over the top of his head at the man behind him and said, "How many dragon ears do you want?"

Sid turned and walked toward the blacksmith shop and another afternoon of hard work and worry.

44

As soon as Cook saw Axel, she curtsied deeply and kept her eyes on the floor.

Axel said, "What's the matter with you this morning, Cook."

Cook wrang her hands and said, "Oh, Your Majesty, I'm so ashamed of the way I been treating you."

"Cook, you've treated. . .What do you mean, Your Majesty?"

Sidney said, as he came through the door, "You being King Axel."

Axel turned and looked into Sidney's eyes and nodded. They'd discuss this when they were alone.

Cook said that they didn't have to come to the kitchen, they could have anything they wanted brought to them anywhere they were.

Sidney said that they would be fine right here, and he and Axel were seated at the table with the bow in front of them when the men of the castle began drifting in. Sir Bruce was one of the first knights to enter the kitchen, and as he did so, said, "Long live the king."

Sir Bruce told them that the king had died in the late afternoon. He greeted Axel with a slight bow and the words, "Good morning, Your Majesty."

Axel was disturbed by this. Not only had he liked King Willard, but he wasn't king yet. He was sure there had to be some kind of ceremony first, and he said so.

Sidney explained, "It doesn't need a ceremony, Your Majesty."

"Sidney, stop that."

"That's the way everyone will talk to you, Your Majesty, and you'll have to get used to it."

"If I'm king will people have to do what I say?"

Sidney nodded and said, "They sure will."

"All right. I ask you to call me Axel."

"Yes, Your Majesty, I'll call you King Axel."

"No more of this, Sidney. You know what I want."

"Sure, Axel. Just kidding."

Sir Bruce was frowning when he said, "Kidding a king?"

"Axel looked at Sir Bruce and asked, "Is it true that there doesn't have to be a ceremony to make me king? I just am one?"

Sir Bruce had been wounded in battle many times. His face was badly scarred, and a long red one ran from his right eye down through the beard on his face to below his upper lip. It was frightening when he looked hard at Axel and said, "Don't you want to be king, Your Majesty?"

Axel didn't answer the large and dominating knight. He didn't have to now that he was the king, did he? He looked at Sidney and said, "What's the process like that makes me king?"

Sidney counted on his fingers the steps. "First you have to be prince. Second, the king has to die or be too sick to carry on. Third, you're automatically the king. It's that simple."

"Why so quick?"

Sir Bruce said in his rough voice, "So we don't do without a king for longer than we have to."

Axel thought that he really didn't have a choice. I guess that's it. I'm king. That must mean that Molly's queen and Sid's prince. I know they won't like that much, and I know I don't, but it looks like we don't have a choice.

171

Looking at Sidney he said, "What do we do about the king?"

"We bury him."

"When?"

"Today."

"So soon?"

Sir Bruce spoke up, "We don't wait a long time when there's any question about who the king is. We have to get rid of the old one as fast as we can."

Axel thought, That doesn't sound so nice, but if that's the way it's done, I guess that's the way it'll have to be.

Sir Bruce had noticed the bow lying on the table, and was very interested in it. When Sidney told him what it could do, Sir Bruce, of course, didn't believe him. Sidney said that there would be a demonstration in the courtyard at noon.

"Sir Bruce," Sidney said, "would you see that the knights and guards will be there?"

The knight looked at Axel and said, "If that's what King Axel wants, I will."

Axel nodded his head.

Sidney smiled as this exchange took place and said, "Everyone is invited, Sir Bruce. The more people who will be there the better it will be for everyone."

The knight frowned when he asked, "Why is that?"

Axel stood and said, "It's what I want, Sir Bruce. Please see to it."

The knight stood without moving for a moment and Axel asked him if there was anything else he needed to know.

"Yes, Your Majesty. I'd like to offer my armor for the test. It's the thickest in the kingdom, and if that bow can shoot an arrow through it, it can go through any armor there is."

Axel said that would be fine and told Sir Bruce to bring just the breastplate with him when he came to the demonstration.

"Yes, Your Majesty," the knight said just before he left the room.

Sidney waited for Axel to sit down and said, "You've got to talk like a king now, Axel."

"What's the matter with the way I talk?"

"It's got to be king-like now."

"How?"

"For instance, you can't say *I*, you have to say *We*."

"Why's that?"

"And you can't say two words as one word, either."

"I don't understand that at all."

"That's a good example of what I mean. You said *I don't*, you have to say *We do not*."

Axel shook his head and said, "That's going to be hard to get used to for we."

"No, it's for *us*."

"All right, for you and we."

"I'm not included in this."

"But. . .you said I had to say *we*."

"You do, but *we* doesn't mean me, too. It means you alone."

"Now that I'm. . .We is king, *We* doesn't mean us, it means me?"

"Yes, but you can't say We is, you have to say We are."

"But if we is just me, that's just one person and I have to say We is, don't I?"

"We'll have to work at this for some time, Axel."

"*We* and *we* will have to."

Sidney frowned and said, "*We and we*? What does that mean?"

"One *We* for me and one *we* for you and me. Isn't that what you said?"

"We'll practice."

"Yes, you and we will."

"It may take time, my boy. . .er. . .King Axel."

There was a parade of guards and knights who stopped in the kitchen for a biscuits and gravy breakfast.

All these men were very interested in the demonstration of the bow. There were heated arguments about whether it would be able to penetrate armor or not.

Some of the knights tried to bend the bow and found that it was so strong that they could hardly move it. They thought that it might be able to send a shaft through heavy steel. Others had no confidence in arrows against their armor. They had seen lots of arrows bounce off their own armor and felt that all arrows would be deflected no matter what shot them.

These arguments were partly because they saw that, if the bow worked like Sidney said it would, it might be a threat to them in the future, and besides, they were interested in any weapon that might give them an edge in battle. This certainly was one that would if it could do what Sidney said it could.

Axel and Sidney agreed that the news of the demonstration would race throughout the castle, and they expected that there would be a crowd at their demonstration. If they were lucky, the spy would be there.

45

Shadows had filled the courtyard and the sky had the last of the evening's glow when the blacksmith put his tools away.

"That's enough for today, Boy. You're a good and hard worker. You keep this up and in another four years or so, you can be a blacksmith just like me."

"Thank you, Sir."

"Be sure and bank the fire good before you quit, Boy." The big man left the shop and disappeared.

Axel was nervous as he carried coal to the forge. He had to be sure no one would see him slip into the wagon or both he and his mother would be caught. He looked out of the front of the shop and the courtyard appeared empty and quiet. Axel took the rag from his face and washed at the bucket.

There was a light in the wagon so his mother was expecting him. He walked directly toward it and stood at the door in back. He knocked softly. No answer. He knocked again. Silence.

"What you want at that wagon, Boy?"

Sid couldn't answer. He couldn't think. He stood and waited to feel hands on him.

"Can't you say?"

Sid turned and looked over his shoulder and there stood one of the two men who had been looking for him yesterday.

Just as he recognized the man, the door opened. Molly saw her son standing below her in the light from the opened door and just beyond him, and walking toward the wagon, was a man saying something to her son.

She couldn't let Sid be caught a second time, especially now when they were so close to escaping. What to do?

Molly forced herself to speak, "I waited a bit for you, Boy. What took you so long? I saved two like you paid me to. Let me take care of this gentleman and I'll get them for you."

Molly lifted her voice over her son's head and said to the man, "What can I do for you, Sir? I'm out of dragon ears, except for the two I promised the blacksmith's boy."

She could see the man lose interest when she said she knew the boy and what he wanted. He turned and walked away. And there stood her son, bathed in the light that showed her his beautiful face.

Molly held out her hand and Sid took it and she pulled him up the stairs and into the wagon. She quickly shut the door and squeezed Sid to her harder than she ever had.

He was home and his mother was holding him. Sid felt safe and wonderful. His mother had saved him just like he knew she would.

Molly opened a chest that was built into the side of the wagon and took out the blankets. Sid stood holding onto her skirt watching what she was doing. He didn't want to let go or to move away from her.

Molly pulled a tab in one corner and the bottom of the chest came up. Below that was another bottom with just a few inches in between. Molly turned and took Sid's face in her hands and kissed him hard and whispered, "In here, quickly, Sid."

Sid jumped in the chest and lay down. Molly told him to turn his face and feet to the side, and she put the false bottom back in place. When the blankets were returned to the top portion of the chest, her son had disappeared. Safe.

Molly hitched the horse to the wagon, put the feed and water buckets away, blew out the lantern and drove to the big gate.

The guard stepped into the light of a lantern hanging over the entrance and held up his hand. When Molly stopped, he asked, "Why so late, Dragon Ears lady?"

"I had to wait for a customer who wanted to pick up his dragon ears later. He came and got them and I'm anxious to get home."

"I thought you people lived in your wagons."

Was this a test? "We do."

"Then you are home. Why you want to leave?"

Molly didn't like the way this conversation was going. She couldn't spend the night in the castle. She had to get Sid out before he was missed. "I have to make the ears for tomorrow. My supplies aren't in this wagon and this oven is too small to make as many as I'll need."

The guard relaxed and laughed. "Then I guess I'll have to let you out, eh?" The guard stood still, looking at Molly. She couldn't think of anything to say and didn't know what he was thinking or why he was hesitating to open the gate.

Finally he spoke, "They sure are good. Any left?"

Now Molly understood what he wanted. She felt great relief, and said, "Not tonight, but I might tomorrow, and if I do, do you want me to save you a couple?"

"Sure do," the guard said, and he began turning the wheel that raised the gate. The screeching of the dry wooden gears echoed in the empty courtyard.

Just behind her, on the off side of the wagon, came a deep voice, sounding as if it were used to being obeyed. "Hold that wheel, guard,"

The screeching stopped. Molly was cold and she was stiff with fear. Were they caught?

There were steps on the other side of the wagon and the heavy and commanding voice again. "Down from the wagon, woman."

When she tied the reins and moved her feet, Molly felt faint and weak, but she did manage to turn and back down from the high seat. None of the men standing watching her difficulty held out a hand to help her. When she was firmly on her feet, she turned and looked at the dark man. His face was lit by the torches burning on either side of the large gate, so his eyes, black patches in his face, reflected the light in small twin spots of yellow.

"Who are you and what are you doing with this Gypsy wagon selling bread?"

What could she say? She couldn't play dumb, although that's what she wanted to do. There was no good reason for one Gypsy wagon to be here while the rest of them were parked by the woods outside Willardville.

Molly opened her mouth to answer. She had no plan and certainly no answer, but she had to say something. Nothing came out. She had no ideas and no words presented themselves of their own accord. She held her hands out to the sides of her body and looked at the man, then dropped her arms and said, "I need to sell my dragon ears."

Rohn moved to her side and examined her carefully in the dim light. His bold eyes were embarrassing and Molly felt shame, though she knew there was no reason to.

This man stood with his back straight and had an assurance that the others did not. He barked at her, "Why are you here when the rest of your people are in Willardville?

The only thing that Molly could think was that maybe she could get him to let her leave if she were in trouble with her fellow Gypsies. She decided to try that. "My people sent me to make money."

"Why?"

Why indeed? Nothing made any sense to her. "They caught me and I have to pay them back," squirted out of her mouth.

Rohn grabbed Molly by the shoulder and squeezed so hard the pain made her faint. He leaned forward so that he was speaking directly into her face. "Caught you doing what, woman? Out with it."

The strong garlic on his breath closed her throat and she pulled backward, away from his black eyes and bad smell.

He reached quickly and grabbed her by the hair and pulled her close and, her hair in his fist, was able to twist her head so that she was looking up over his left shoulder.

She kicked out with her foot and caught Rohn hard on the shin. He barked once and released her hair. But now Molly felt her arms pinned from behind and again she was forced to stand in front of this frightening man. Molly looked at the ground. This was easier, for she didn't have to look at those dark eyes.

Rohn grabbed her chin and forced her to look at him. "Answer me, wench."

Molly's voice was small even to her ears when she said, "I stole money from the wagon of the leader. I have to pay him back."

179

The men standing by the wagon laughed and Molly, even knowing it was a lie, was embarrassed by the admission.

The large, dark man held up his hand for silence and instantly there was no more laughter. "Search this wagon, guard. Let's make sure this woman hasn't stolen from us, too."

Molly turned and looked up at Rohn and said, "I'm just trying to pay back what I owe. I have to get this wagon back as soon as I can. Let me go," and she squirmed in the guard's grip.

Rohn said, "Let's see what she has in there. You two," and he pointed at two guards, "search the wagon. We're looking for a boy."

Molly's heart broke. They were so close to getting away. She had been excited to think that she had Sid back and now they were going to find him and they'd never get another chance. It wasn't fair. She loved him more than her life and had worked so hard to free him.

Molly couldn't protest. It would give Sid away if she objected to a search. She had to stand quietly and hope as hard as she could that the two men would miss the false bottom in the trunk.

The wagon sagged when the men climbed in. She could hear them as they moved things around and opened doors and cupboards. There were short periods of silence then soft banging and thumps, then silence again. The wagon shifted on its springs as the men moved. There was a short silent period, but it was interrupted by a sharp cry from inside the wagon.

46

That morning they buried King Willard, and that's all the funeral there was. They just put him in a box and put it in the ground in the graveyard next to the temple. Axel was surprised that there wasn't a big ceremony. Everyone was there, but that's all they did.

Axel and Sidney spent the next two hours in the woods next to town practicing with the bow. They wanted to make sure they knew how to aim it, for they didn't want to miss the armor with it during the test. Axel had wanted Sidney to conduct the test because the bow was his invention. Sidney thought that would be better than having the king do the test.

They set a breastplate against a tree and stepped back about fifty feet. Sidney pulled the lever that drew back the string, cocking the bow. There must have been tremendous tension, because, even with the help of the lever, the bow was very hard to cock.

Sidney sighted down the shaft, held the bow as steady as he could and pulled the firing lever. The arms of the bow snapped forward, the string sang and the arrow disappeared.

The men couldn't find the arrow in the tree or in the ground around it. It had to be somewhere, but where?

"Let's do it again, Sidney."

"*Let us* do it again."

"I just said that."

"Not that way."

"I did, too."

"*We* did, too."

"I know. I just heard you say it after I said it. We both said it."

Sidney said, "This is going to be harder than I thought."

"We don't know that. Let's shoot another arrow. We might hit the armor next time.

"You know I didn't mean the shot."

"I thought you were really trying."

"I was."

"But you said. . ."

"Let's stop playing around and I'll shoot another arrow."

"You mean *we* should shoot another arrow?"

"No, I'll do it."

"I thought you said that *we* meant one person now."

"Just for you, Axel."

"Now that we is a king?"

Sidney looked into Axel's eyes for a long moment, shook his head slowly and said, "Right."

Sidney worked the lever that forced the string back against the pull of the arms, put a shaft in the groove on the top of the board that held the bow and fitted it on the string.

This time he moved to within twenty-five feet of the armor before he shot again.

They both heard the chunk of the arrow striking the metal. When they examined the breastplate, they found a hole. The arrow had gone completely through the metal and buried itself in the tree.

Sidney danced and Cynthia, still mostly plucked and singed, clung swaying and bouncing on his shoulder. Sidney and his bird performed a strange ritual there in the clearing. The mostly bald man, dressed in his new black cloak with stars on it and with a nearly featherless chicken on his shoulder, danced by himself and sang.

The wizard made a brand new bow
To shoot and make all Rohn's men go
Back to where they should have stayed
Where they belong and not here strayed.

Right through their armor arrows go
And this will let Rohn's army know
That I have planned and haven't played.
A great new bow this wizard made.

Axel clapped his hands and laughed when Sidney sat at the base of the tree, winded but excited. "Well done, Sidney."

"Thank you, Axel. I deserve the praise."

Both men were feeling good having succeeded and relaxed against the tree. But in a moment, Axel was troubled by the thought that there could have been a man in back of that armor.

Axel sat upright and said, "Sidney, we have to make sure the demonstration fails."

Rolling his head on the trunk so that he could look at Axel, Sidney asked, "What are you talking about?"

"If the knights see what this thing can do, they'll know that their armor won't protect them if they face an enemy who has bows like it. It will do away with armor."

"And?"

"Instead of knights battling for honor and justice, they'll just be killing each other. There'll be men hacking at each other with axes just like the barbarians do. Axel saw in his mind rows of men with the new bow facing an army that was a long way away. Too far for the enemy's bows to be effective. The men with the new bows shoot and the arrows fly and kill the enemy and they're too far away to fight back. A slaughter.

"We have to hide what this bow can do, Sidney."

Sidney stood and looked toward the castle. Axel rose and stood next to him trying to see what he was looking at.

"We can do that, Axel, but you're not thinking of Sid now. We've made this bow for him and the people in Willardville and for the kingdom. You're the king now, remember. You can't think just about yourself. You have to think of everyone when you make decisions. You may not like it, but there it is."

Axel could feel the pressure of what Sidney said pushing down on him. It was almost as if his words were weights making him feel heavy. He could see in his mind Sid, and then he could see the castle and the town, then Sid and then the town. Did it have to be one or the other? Why not both?

"Sidney, I can't turn my back on my responsibility to the kingdom, but I have one to my son, too."

"It will almost always be this way, Axel."

"With responsibilities that conflict with each other?"

"Almost always."

"What do I do?"

"What you have to do based on a set of values you accept."

Axel had thought about this but asked, "How does that work?"

"This gets complicated here. You have to decide on what basis you're going to make decisions before you start making them."

Axel thought about that and said, "Give me an example."

It took Sidney a while to come up with one. When he did, he turned and looked into Axel's eyes and said, "Suppose you decided that you should do the most good for the largest number of people. That would mean that you would have to make decisions based on that value."

Axel was quiet as he thought about that, then he said, "In that case, if I used that value, I'd make this decision for the kingdom and not for Sid."

"Yes. That's what it means. Now, if you had the value based on doing the thing that would make you the happiest for the moment, it would mean that you might make a different decision."

"I can see that."

"Suppose you had a value that said that the most important thing was your power. In that case you'd decide on the kingdom. Using the bow would make you a hero with a very strong army."

Axel walked away into the trees to be by himself. Sidney again sat with his face turned to the sun and closed his eyes. It was out of his hands now.

When Axel returned, Sidney was asleep. Axel shook him by the shoulder and said, "Let's go, Sidney. It must be almost noon."

The courtyard was full of men waiting for the demonstration. When Axel and Sidney walked through the gate, the crowd cheered and yelled in celebration. Axel turned to look at Sidney as if to ask what it was all about, and Sidney said to him out of the side of his mouth, "They're cheering the new king, Axel."

Axel remembered, "Oh, yes. I almost forgot in the excitement of the test."

47

The courtyard was jammed with people wanting to see the demonstration. The knights had done a good job of telling people that something exciting was going on.

Sir Bruce met Axel and Sidney by the arched entrance to the great room. He had his breastplate with him and held it out to Sidney. Sidney had the bow and said, "Take the armor, will you, Axel?"

Axel could hear the knights suck in their breath. Was the wizard talking to the new king that way? Not only did he call the king Axel but he told him to do something. Maybe we should have his head for it. We'll see what the king does. He should take care of it easily.

Reaching, Axel held his hand out for the breastplate. Sir Bruce couldn't believe what was happening and didn't respond, so Axel made a motion with his fingers, and the knight handed him the piece of steel. Axel carried it into the courtyard behind Sidney. The knights had never seen anything like this, and they watched silently their new king carrying a knight's armor.

The crowd parted before a post that had been set into the hard ground. Sidney led the way to it and Axel followed with the breastplate. The wizard pushed on the post with his hand to check how steady it was, then looked past it to see where the arrow might go. Satisfied, he motioned for Axel to put the armor against it.

Axel stepped forward and hung the breastplate on the pole, then both men walked back about twenty-five feet. The crowd circled them except behind the target.

There was no noise in the courtyard at all. Everyone was too concentrated on what was going on to talk.

Sidney cocked the bow, took aim and waited. The suspense built. When he felt the tension was as great as it was going to get, he fired. There was the expected twang of the string and the chunk of the arrow going through steel, but this time the arrow also passed through the post and was sticking out the far side of it with just the feathers hidden in the wood.

The crowd was too astonished to speak. None of them had ever seen anything like this. This was too great an event to talk about. The nearly impossible had happened right in front of them.

The bell began ringing. At the sound, the men all looked toward the tower where it hung. They waited for some sign, some explanation for its alarm. The courtyard was quiet until a man ran from the great room yelling, "Rohn's coming, Rohn's army is on the march. It's war with Rohn. To arms. To arms."

48

Everyone looked at Axel to see what he'd tell them to do. This was his first test as king and how would he act? He knew that he was in control and the knights would take their lead from him. If he acted scared, they would be. If he acted relaxed, it would calm them.

Axel thought that this would be best. He motioned to Sir Bruce to come and stand next to him. As the leader of the knights, he was the one Axel had to deal with.

Axel said very casually to huge knight, "Have your best archer practice with the new bow. When he can hit what he aims at, have him report to me. Next, find out how far away Rohn's men are."

Sir Bruce, looking straight ahead, said, "Yes, Your Majesty."

Axel looked where the knight was looking, expecting to see the king. He caught himself just before he asked where the king was and told Sir Bruce to come with him.

Axel led the way. He was followed by Grrr, Sidney and Sir Bruce. When they were seated in the great room, Axel said, "We have a problem."

Sidney smiled, the knight nodded his head. "This is what we'll do to solve it. Sidney, you have the carpenters make twenty bows."

"Axel, there isn't time for that."

Sir Bruce's mouth fell open and he looked to see what the king would do about being called Axel.

"They don't have to work, Sidney. They only have to look like they might. From a distance it has to look as if we have twenty of the new bows, and if we have to we can kill all of the knights with the first volley."

Sidney's unlined face lit with understanding and he grinned and said, "Yes, Your Majesty,"

"Then I want you to get someone to make another twenty, but these don't have to look much like the first twenty. These can be just crossed pieces of wood. They'll be held by men on the battlements of the castle. They'll have to look like the new bow from the road that runs past the castle."

Sidney was laughing as he ran through the arched doorway to the courtyard and turned toward the carpentry shop, yelling out as he ran, "The king needs ten men to help the carpenter. You men there, follow me."

Axel turned to face his head knight and said, "Sir Bruce, after you have reported to me on the first two things I asked of you, I want you to find a place somewhere on the road that runs past the castle where you can position ten men hidden on each side. They should be placed so that they will have a clear shot at the leading knights. They should be about twenty feet apart so that it will look as if Rohn's knights will have a gauntlet of new bows to get through.

"When you have picked the spot, return to me and report." Axel didn't wait for the knight to respond, he continued, "Here is what else you can do to help. Get one of the knights to find whoever it is who makes flags or sheets or clothes or does the best sewing in the castle and have them make a very big cloth sign that says, *Welcome Duke Rohn*. Now, this has to be big enough to stretch clear across the roadway. Find someone to put poles in the ground and string this sign up high enough that a man on a horse can ride under it." Axel waited and the knight nodded and said, "Yes, Your Majesty."

49

When Axel walked into the very busy courtyard, he realized that the castle was preparing for a siege. The bell had been ringing steadily since the message had first come about Rohn's approach, and the courtyard was full of people running and shouting. Men were carrying woven baskets of arrows to the slitted windows in the towers and up the ramps to the embrasures in the parapets. Men were stacking pikes against the banquettes that ran around the castle walls. There were fires being built in pits on the wall overlooking the drawbridge and large vats of oil were being heated. Axel had learned when the blue men invaded that if invaders were to try to batter down the raised drawbridge, the king's men would pour boiling oil on them.

People from town were rushing to the castle. The men carrying pitchforks and scythes, the women carrying children and as much clothing as they could. Again the guards wouldn't let them bring carts past the drawbridge, so there were a great many left by the side of the road leading to the castle. There was a group of men pushing them over the cliffs into the sea.

Cattle and sheep were being driven through the gates, and with all the townspeople coming inside, there was a great deal of confusion, noise and clouds of dust.

Axel stopped a knight and said, "What is your name?" The knight was surprised that the new king had spoken to him, but he was pleased, "Fallon, Your Majesty."

"Sir Fallon, here's what I need you to do. Get two other knights to help you and go outside the main gate and tell the townspeople to stop coming into the castle. Have them set up tables outside the gates, just on the other side of the moat. They are to put food and drink on the tables, as for a feast. Can you organize that?"

The knight didn't understand why the king would want anything so strange done, but he was the king and what he wanted was what got done. He said, "Yes, Your Majesty, I'll do it now," and he hurried off.

Axel stopped another knight who was being suited up in his armor, and said to this man, "What is your name?"

Also pleased, the knight answered, "Sir John, Your Majesty."

"Sir John, I need you to do something for me. Can you help?"

What a surprise, the king asking a knight if the knight would help. The knight was almost unable to speak, but did manage to croak out, "Yes, Your Majesty."

"First, take off the armor. I want you to gather four other knights and hide all of this preparation for war. The arms can be left on the parapets, but they should not be visible from the courtyard or from the front of the castle. Have the men with the oil pots shield them from view. Have some workmen erect tents on the road that goes past the castle. Have flags flown over them just like when there is a celebration or a fair. Direct these townspeople back out of the courtyard. Have them help set up the tables." The knight frowned as if he didn't understand. "Do you understand?"

"Yes, Your Majesty. Should I do that now, Sire?"

Axel was turning away and nodded his head and the knight ran off. Glancing at the tower, Axel frowned and stopped a soldier and said to him, "Tell that bellman to stop ringing the bell." The man ran toward the stairs that led to the tower.

When Axel stood in the center of the courtyard, he noticed that it was a good bit less busy now that the townspeople were no longer streaming in. He walked to the big gate and watched people setting up tables and putting the food on them that they had brought to the castle for the siege.

A man carrying Sidney's new bow ran up to Axel, removed his hat and stood looking at the ground. Axel said, "Look at me, Bowman." The man hesitated, probably from fear, then looked at his king's face. Axel smiled and didn't say anything. So strange, but the man tried a smile himself. Then both men were grinning.

Axel put his hand on the man's shoulder and said, "Can you hit what you aim for, good soldier?"

I've tried this wonderful bow. It hits what I want it to, Your Majesty."

Axel glanced around to see that none of the people moving through the courtyard could hear them and said, "There is a very important thing that you can do for your king and your people. Are you ready for it?"

"I'll do whatever you ask, Your Majesty."

"I knew I could count on you," Axel said, looking the man in the eyes and smiling. "We only have the one bow you've been working with, but we want Rohn and his men to think that we have many. It is important they think that we can kill the armored knights whenever we want to. Do you understand?"

The man nodded and said, "Yes, Your Majesty."

"When Rohn's men get here, you and I will be in the center of the road, right at the near end of the twenty bowmen who will be on either side. We'll demonstrate for Rohn what this bow can do. He will think that all twenty can do the same.

192

"I'll ask Rohn to get me a breastplate from one of his knights. I'll put it in the road in front of Rohn and you have to put an arrow through it. This has to be just a one-shot try. You can't miss. Can you do that?"

"I'll try, Your Majesty."

Axel shook his head. "Not good enough. We will have but one chance. Rohn won't give a second. You have to be sure. Sir Bruce said you were the best bowman in the castle. If you cannot do it, who can?"

The soldier stood straight, and looking Axel in the eye, said, "I'm the best and I can do it in one shot."

Axel put his hand back on the man's shoulder, gave it a squeeze and looking into his eyes, said, "I trust you. I think you will shoot through the armor in one shot.

"When you hear that Rohn's men are on the road that goes past the castle to Willardville, meet me where the road to the castle meets it. Can you do that?"

"I'll be there, Your Majesty."

"Bring that bow and be sure you have two arrows with you."

The bowman smiled and said, "I can hit the armor with the first try. I won't need two, Your Majesty."

Looking into the man's eyes, Axel said, "The second one is for Rohn if the first one doesn't work."

Rohn? thought the bowman. How strange. He demonstrates the bow, plans a picnic and then kills the Duke. This king is hard to understand.

"Now this is important, listen carefully. I'm going to tell Rohn that we have bows that can shoot arrows through not only his knight's armor but then through the knights bodies and out their back armor. He won't believe me. That's fine. I'll then tell him that I'm ready to demonstrate. This is when you will have to do your job. We will all be counting on you."

There, Axel thought, I may have condemned a man to death. I did what Sidney told me to do. I picked a value and made this decision based on it.

I've the value of not killing, but the second one I have, to protect my family, is a greater value. When they're in conflict, the greater value is the one I keep first.

I know I'll suffer if I cause Rohn to die, but if it saves Molly and Sid's lives and all the lives in the castle, it'll be a decision well made. Axel turned to look at the entrance to see how the food tables were being set up and Sir Bruce was standing in front of him.

"Your Majesty, Rohn's army is about three hours away to the north."

"Very well, Sir Bruce."

The knight didn't move. Axel said, "Anything else?"

"Yes, Your Majesty. I have selected a spot for the archers."

"Show me."

Sir Bruce told a workman standing nearby to select two horses, saddle them and take them to the gate. Leading the way, Axel and his head knight wove through people and animals toward the gate. Just then the bell stopped ringing, and Axel glanced up at the tower and nodded his head. Things were working out the way they should. Axel hadn't had a chance yet to think about King Willard dying, but he knew that would come.

He had a lot to think about when he had the time. What would Molly think about being a queen and Sid think about being a prince? What would he think about being King Axel? That alone will take me some time to work out, he thought. I might have to talk to Sidney about it.

But now he had much to do. He was standing at the entrance when a stable boy came leading two horses. Axel and Sir Bruce mounted and thundered over the bridge and moat.

They rode down the narrow spine of land. Once away from the entrance where the tables had been set up, the top of the cliff was so narrow that it was hard to be comfortable riding side by side. It had been built this way so that siege engines would have trouble reaching the big door, and any army which attacked could send up only four or five men abreast at a time.

Near the junction of the road to the castle and the road to Willardville, men were setting posts, one on each side of the road. Axel knew they were for the banner. On both sides of the road south of the banner, men were erecting the tents Axel had ordered.

50

Axel and Sir Bruce turned north when they reached the corner where the road turned toward the castle, and rode for only thirty or forty yards before the knight said, "Here, Your Majesty."

Axel halted his horse. There were shallow ditches and bushes on both sides of the roadway. "How far down this road is it the same as it is here?"

"Another hundred yards, Your Majesty."

Axel urged his horse forward and examined both sides of the road. When he had ridden about a hundred yards, he said to Sir Bruce, "You have chosen well, good knight. When we get the message that Rohn's men are just on the far side of that hill ahead, station your men here about twenty feet apart. Keep them out of sight until I signal." Axel indicated both sides of the road.

Riding back to the branch in the road, Axel pointed to a spot right at the junction and said, "Here is where I'll be waiting with the bowman. Where we'll demonstrate the bow for Rohn.

"I've heard that Rohn has fewer than twenty knights in armor, and the twenty bowmen should give them something serious to think about."

Sir Bruce didn't know if he should correct the king, but he had to be sure that his men weren't slaughtered, too. He decided to take a chance. "But, Sire, we don't have twenty bows. We only have the one that was used in the demonstration."

"Rohn doesn't know that. At that point he should agree with me that we all eat lunch instead of killing each other."

This astonished the knight. Eat with Rohn? He wasn't sure that Axel being king was such a good idea after all. When the king had adopted him, Sir Bruce was in favor of it, for he knew that Axel had cleared the kingdom of dragons and later of the blue men. But lunch on a battlefield?

"What happens if he doesn't agree to have lunch, Your Majesty?"

"That's the other reason I'll have the bowman with me. I've told him to bring two arrows. The first for the demonstration, the second for Rohn if he's not hungrier than he is mad.

"When he's seen what the bow can do, he may still not be convinced that war is not the answer for him. At that point I'll raise my hand. The bowman will kill Rohn at my signal, and the twenty bowmen will stand up from the ditches and come from behind the bushes and aim at the knights."

The knight thought about that for a bit and nodded his head. Not a bad idea after all.

The sky had turned dark with low clouds and now there was a fine snow driven by the wind from the sea. It hadn't covered the ground yet, but Axel knew it soon would. That might give him a problem. The men in the ditches would make tracks when they left the road and got behind the bushes.

"Sir Bruce."

"Yes, Sire."

"One further thing. It's starting to snow." Axel was looking carefully at the line of bushes on the sea side of the road.

Doesn't this new king think I can't see it's snowing? He lifted his head and look about him with concentration and said, "Yes, Your Majesty, I believe it is."

"Rohn and his men mustn't know there are men behind the bushes. They can't leave tracks in the snow. If we need those men, their being there has to be a surprise."

The knight liked that idea and smiled to himself. "They can come up to the road from the fields in back of the rows of bushes."

Axel looked carefully at the fields on both sides of the road. On the sea side, there was a shelf of flat, wind-swept rock. On the other side, there was a narrow band of wild field and then dark woods, the tree trunks black against the light swirling snow.

"Yes, Sir Bruce, good idea. Have the archers do that."

51

Just as Axel and Sir Bruce turned and headed back to the castle, they heard the sounds of hoofbeats on the dry roadway. Turning in their saddles and looking over their shoulders, they saw a horseman followed by a plume of dust and snow riding hard down the hill to the north.

"That may be the scout making a report on Rohn. Let's wait here for him," Axel said as he turned his horse to face the hill and the wind.

The scout rode his horse hard to the king and Sir Bruce and reigned in it harshly in front of them.

"Easy on that horse, Soldier," Axel said.

The man and his horse were both breathing hard, their breath white plumes that blew away as soon as they formed. "Your Majesty, I could see Rohn's men from the crest of that hill. They may be three miles north of there.

"How many knights in armor and where are they?"

"They were too far away to count, Sire, but I could see the shine of armor and the road was full of men as far as I could see. At least another mile back."

Rohn has come prepared for a long siege, Axel thought, or he figures that I'll give up when I see the power of his army. King Willard's men won't stand much of a chance in battle against him if this plan doesn't work.

Sir Bruce said, "Should we warn the castle? Your Majesty?"

Axel heard his knight speaking over the sounds of horses and men screaming. "Yes, Sir Bruce. Warn the castle and start the bowmen down into that woods and along the cliff and tell them about tracks when they get close to the road." The knight raced off toward the castle, and Axel rode with the scout and his blowing horse.

Before Axel and the soldier reached the big gate, a line of men ran from the castle and down the spine of land that formed the road to it. They were carrying bows like Sidney's bow. They even had strings on them. Sidney's carpenters had done a good job, for they looked just like the original. Each man even had three or four of the short arrows stuck in his belt.

Axel watched as the men split into two groups when they reached the road. Some crossed the road and ran into the woods, others turned toward the cliff and ran along the stone edge. When they reached the place where they were to station themselves, one by one they disappeared into the bushes that lined the roadway.

In a moment the countryside was as empty of people as it had been during the dragon infestations. But there was activity near the castle—people moving around the tables, setting out plates of food. It looked strange to Axel to have people planning on eating outdoors in the snow, but this whole day had been strange.

He rode into the castle and a stableboy took his horse and Axel said, "Saddle Charger for me, Boy." He looked over the courtyard. All preparation for war was gone. The courtyard looked just as it always did. The blacksmith was working. He could hear the hammer pounding something. The workshops had people in them working. A day like any other.

Sidney had been in the kitchen but came out to the courtyard just as Axel stepped out of the stable. He was carrying Axel's battle sword, the one that Sir Bruce had given him. When he saw Axel, he waved and the men walked toward each other. Axel spoke first, "Sidney, what are you doing with my sword?"

"I brought it to you, Axel. If there's fighting, you'll need it."

"Put it back," Axel said and he gestured toward the great room.

"But—"

"If I need it, it'll be too late to use it. But if I don't have it with me, I'll have to use my mind, and I'm better with that than I'll ever be with a sword." Axel smiled to take the sting out of his refusal to take the sword and to let his friend know that he appreciated his thinking. "Sidney, is the bowman Sir Bruce selected ready?"

"He's sure he is, Axel. He's in the kitchen talking to Cook. He's nervous, but he's the best we got."

"Ask him to come out. It's time he and I went to the road and got in position."

Sidney headed for the arch leading to the great room, and Axel crossed the courtyard to the stable to get Charger. When he was mounted, he rode to the gate and halted his horse beside the man whose job it was to raise and lower the big door, Axel said to him, "You are doing a fine job here, soldier." The man was so flustered that this new king had spoken to him that he couldn't make himself speak. Axel waited, but when the man only looked at him, he went on, "I do not want you to raise the drawbridge unless I am killed. Do you understand what I want?" The man nodded and Axel leaned down and put his hand on the man's shoulder and patted him gently. "I know you do, good soldier."

When he crossed the huge door that formed the bridge over the moat and looked to his right, Axel could see, just coming over the crest of the distant hill in a gauze of swirling snow, a line of men on horseback.

201

Rohn's army had arrived and in a few minutes they would be at the bottom of the hill.

"I'm ready, Sire." the voice behind him said.

Axel jerked at the sound so close to him. He was much more nervous that he'd supposed he could get. When he turned, the bowman straightened in his saddle and said again, "Your Majesty, I have two arrows and I'm confident that I can hit the armor on the first shot."

"I am, too, bowman. It's time we got to the road and waited for our guests."

The soldier looked around them and said, "Are we going down there alone, Your Majesty?"

"Yes."

"Is it safe for us. . .you, to expose yourself this way, Your Majesty?"

"Come," Axel said as he started over the bridge.

The two men watched the army inching down the far hill. The armored knights were in the lead, riding two abreast on the flat roadway. In front of the knights were three riders carrying standards with white flags riding stiffly in the wind. The knights were in polished armor with white trappings and the one in the lead was all in black. I wonder if that's Rohn? Axel asked himself. That's pretty strange to have your knights in white and silver and be in black yourself.

When they reached the road, Axel and the bowman stationed themselves in the center between the ditches. Axel said loudly enough for the men lying in the bushes to hear, "Don't move or make a sound until I raise my hand and this bowman kills Rohn. You are here to be used only if necessary. I hope we don't need you at all. If not, stay down and out of sight."

52

It was hard to stand still in the empty road and wait for the advancing army. The bowman was shifting in his saddle and fiddling with the bow. Axel said gently, "Be still, bowman. You don't want them to think you're nervous or scared." The bowman was comforted by the king's calm voice and sat still.

The standard bearers in front of the knights were just entering Willardville and would be in front of Axel and the bowman in about twenty minutes. Axel could now hear the beat of a large drum. The sound came to him through the muffling of the snow, and the cadence was slow, slower than the steps of a man walking. The effect, as intended, was to make enemies nervous.

The column was now about one hundred yards away. Axel was looking at Rohn, at least he thought that was the man dressed in black. He couldn't let that man see him turning and talking to anyone. Continuing to stare straight ahead, Axel said, "Bowman, do not look at anything but the man in black. You will see my arm as movement if I raise it, but concentrate your eyes on the target. You may not get time later to refocus on him."

Axel knew that if Rohn's men killed their new king, his knights would close up the castle and fight. That would mean that they all would die. Everyone in the castle. There weren't enough men in the castle to defend it against Rohn. And, he hadn't allowed the stock that had been brought inside the walls to stay. The animals had been herded back to the farms, so there wasn't enough food in the castle to stand much of a siege.

His plan worked or they all were dead. "Bowman. I do not want you to say anything. You are not to touch me or Charger. You are not to look at me. Look only at the knight in black. No matter what happens, do not move or speak. Do you understand how important this is?"

"Yes, Your Majesty."

Axel wanted to giggle. Strangers calling him 'Your Majesty'. If the situation weren't so serious, he'd have to laugh at how absurd it all was. He had been a poor farmer's son and now, just a few years later, he was a king. Axel did smile, and that made him laugh. He put his head back and laughed till tears ran down his face. He released much of his tension by that and it make him feel better and almost calm.

The approaching men were close enough by then to see Axel smile and hear him laugh. That may have been good for Axel. It might mean that this upstart wasn't worried or he wouldn't laugh and smile. That must have bothered Rohn. He couldn't have understood why Axel wasn't afraid.

The army Axel was facing was much bigger than his own. He had no chance of winning a fight. When they rode past Willardville, he had seen the stock still in the fields and in the barns. So they couldn't have enough food in the castle to withstand a siege.

Rohn knew that something was going on here that he didn't understand. He'd have to think about this very carefully. This Axel knew something that made him confident. But what?

The standard bearers halted their horses at the side of the road, and Rohn continued toward Axel until he was right in front of him. After pushing up the visor on his helmet with the back of one gauntletted hand, he sat stiffly in the saddle and didn't move or speak but stared into Axel's eyes. Axel didn't move either and stared back.

Rohn's black beard and mustache hid most of his face, but from what he could see, Axel recognized a slight resemblance to King Willard. After all, they were brothers.

This went on for almost a minute. Black eyes and light green ones locked. Axel couldn't do this for long, but Rohn looked away from Axel's eyes and examined the bowman to Axel's left and then the banner. They studied the narrow track to the castle. Axel could see their movement stop when Rohn saw the tables of food standing by the gate in the blowing snow.

The big man in black frowned and looked back at Axel. This might be good, Axel thought. He thinks we're very confident about something. We didn't meet him with a line of charging knights. There aren't thousands of arrows in the air. There is no threat. We're just here and not worried. This is the way I wanted this to work.

Rohn spoke, "I have come to take my rightful place as king. Step aside and I may let you live."

Axel saw Rohn's eyes flick to the bowman and back to his own. Axel didn't move.

Rohn waited. The drumming stopped. The wind blew the snow in swirls around them. No one moved.

Grrr must have sensed the tension in the exchange for he stood and leaned forward, his ruff standing up.

Axel said, "We have something to show you, Sir Rohn. We think you will be interested."

Rohn smiled. What could this farmer have that would be worth looking at? "Show me," he said in a soft and confident voice.

Axel nodded his head and said, "We will need the breastplate from the best armor your knights have. Have your man put it there on the ground between us."

Rohn didn't move. There was a long pause as if he were thinking about what trickery might be going on. Finally he nodded and motioned to the first knight behind him to come forward. "Take off your breastplate and place it there in the road facing this man." He nodded at Axel.

Without hesitation, the knight swung off his saddle. It was hard for he had no help and he hit the ground with his feet very solidly. He removed his helmet and then the top of his armor. He placed it in the road and stepped back to his horse and looked at Rohn.

Axel looked at his bowman. The man was frozen. He couldn't move. He must have been so scared his muscles wouldn't work. Axel said gently, "Are you ready, Bowman?"

The man didn't answer. Axel waited as long as he could and then held out his hand for the bow. The bowman looked at Axel's eyes but didn't move. Axel said just as quietly, Give us the bow."

When there was no reaction from the man, Axel reached over and tugged the bow from his stiff fingers and said, "Thank you, Bowman," and gestured for an arrow.

Axel looked at Rohn and said, "It might be good if you had your horse step aside, Sir Rohn. These new bows we have are very powerful. We have developed them so that they can easily penetrate the best armor there is. I know you will be interested in this demonstration, but I would not want you to be hurt."

Rohn laughed and said, "There isn't an arrow that can touch a knight when he's in armor. What you say is just silly," and he looked into Axel's eyes and continued, "or a lie."

Axel smiled and dismounted. Rohn also stepped off his horse. Since he was in armor, this was a difficult thing to do without help, but the big man managed it without staggering. Axel stepped back a few feet and said, "Sir Rohn, please step back here with me."

The knight who had donated his armor, loosened his sword in its scabbard and started to move toward Axel. Rohn held up his hand and said, "No. Stay there."

Axel, followed by Rohn, walked away from the piece of armor till they were about twenty five feet from it. The bowman had led his horse to the side of the road and the field was clear for Axel to shoot the arrow.

But he had never done it before, he'd only seen Sidney shoot it. He wasn't even sure how to force the string back to the trigger bar. He knew that it had to be done with the lever. He'd seen that done, and he knew that the shaft of the arrow had to go in the groove after it was cocked. But that was all. He didn't know how to aim it or to hold it or have any confidence that he could hit anything with it.

Rohn was standing next to Axel watching him fiddling with the bow. "It doesn't look like any bow I've ever seen. Such short arms. It couldn't be as powerful as you say," he said and smiled.

Axel was having trouble getting the lever to pull the string back. It just wasn't working.

He felt pressure on his arm, and when he turned, he saw the bowman was standing next to him holding his hand out for the bow.

Axel looked at Rohn and said, "This bowman will show you what our new bows can do," and he stepped to the side.

With steady hands, the bowman worked the lever and brought the string back against the trigger bar. The arms were bent severely back and looked to be in great strain.

He placed one of the short arrows in the groove and knocked it onto the string. Glancing once at Axel, who nodded, he took aim and there was the sound of the string vibrating and the chunk of the arrow hitting armor.

Axel didn't move, for he could see the hole in the breastplate from where he was standing. The arrow wasn't visible, probably buried in the dirt of the road.

Rohn walked to the armor and picked it up. He looked first at the front with its neat round hole, then he looked at the back and saw another one just like it.

He looked at Axel, frowning like he couldn't believe what he had seen or didn't understand it.

Out of the side of one eye, Axel could see the bowman moving and knew he'd be ready for the second shot if there had to be one.

Rohn dropped the armor and walked closer to Axel and said, "You have bows this powerful and I've never heard of them? How could that be?"

The hair was standing on Grrr's back.

Axel smiled and shrugged his shoulders. Not a kingly thing to do, but he was so relieved that the demonstration had gone as planned that he wasn't worried about appearances.

Axel said to the bowman in a very low voice so that Rohn couldn't hear him. "Do not shoot the second arrow yet." He lifted his arm and men stood up on both sides of the road. They were about fifteen feet apart and had bows like the one that had just put an arrow clean through the best armor in Rohn's army.

Each of the men at the sides of the road had his bow aimed at a knight. Rohn hadn't expected this and his mouth hung open when the bowmen stood. He swung his head back to Axel and hissed, "A trick; you're not the prince and you'll never be king."

Axel was concentrating on the force before him. His mind was working as well and as fast as it ever had. He was acutely aware of the sounds of men near him shifting in their saddles, making the leather squeak in the cold, and swords touching shields making metallic clinks, clear in the snowy air. The sharp smell of the hundreds of nervous horses and frightened men facing him was strong and heavy. His skin was sensitive to the feel of snowflakes melting on it or landing on his eyelashes and remaining until he blinked.

All down the long line of soldiers there were slight movements as if the column were alive and hungry, a breathing, pulsing, deadly, mile long carnivore.

The knights were alternating their attention between Rohn and the men standing in the ditches with the strange bows.

It was so still that Axel could hear the snapping of the flags on the tents behind him and even the dull thumping and slap of the banner as it filled and luffed when it caught and emptied in the wind.

53

Molly and Sid had been taken to the room beneath the castle and both were chained to the wall. They had spent the night huddled together for warmth, and it felt good to both of them to hold and be held.

When there was a light gray in the small opening high in the wall, the prisoners knew that they had survived the night. It had been hard to sleep, but Molly and Sid were exhausted from the previous day's work and being caught when they thought they would escape.

Sid was the first to hear the thump and scrape of the old man who was the jailer. He said to his mother, "Mother, the man's coming to take the slops bucket and leave us water and some bread."

Molly brushed the hair from Sid's forehead and asked, "How do you know?"

"I've been here before and I remember the sound of his feet. Listen and you can hear that he takes one step and then drags his other foot along the floor. It makes a sliding noise that I remember."

Molly reached for her son and held him. She didn't know if Axel even knew she was in Rohn's castle. He sure didn't know where Sid was. He could find out from the Gypsies when she took the wagon and which way she went. She remembered talking with Axel about coming here and selling dragon ears and trying to find out about Sid. Besides, she'd thought he might prevent her from trying if he'd known when she was going.

The two prisoners heard the metallic sounds of the key in the lock and knew they had company. When their cell door swung open, it wasn't the old man who came in first, it was Rohn, the large, dark man who had questioned Molly at the gate.

Molly stood. She didn't want to look up so sharply when he talked to them. Sid stood next to her and they waited for the dark man to speak.

"You just wait till my father learns what you did to us," Sid said. Molly was afraid for him for speaking so boldly and proud of him that he had.

Rohn smiled and said to Molly. "I couldn't learn what your husband is planning on doing about this silly thing of his being adopted by King Willard. Either the boy is very stubborn or doesn't know. That doesn't matter now. I don't care what he has in mind.

"You, on the other hand," Rohn stepped close to Molly and talked right into her face. "will tell me what I need to know about the preparations the king's knights are making, and if they will resist my taking the throne."

"I'll never tell you a thing," Molly said with as much conviction in her voice as she was able to produce. She wasn't sure it was much, chained to the wall as she was, but it was the best she could do.

Rohn smiled, "Oh, I think you'll tell me anything I want to know. I'll give you some time to think about it. I've got some business with my army in the morning, but that shouldn't take long. Once we're set up for the siege, I may stop back for that visit.

"I'll leave you here with the knowledge that when I return, I may talk to you again. One of my guards will be working just down the hall with the boy at the same time. You should be able to hear him screaming as we talk.

"You may be lucky. I may not need to know what you know about which of the king's knights will be loyal to tradition and me and which won't.

54

The king and the would-be-king faced each other in the road with wind-blown snow swirling at their feet.

Axel spoke clearly and directly into the dark eyes, "I am not a prince. I am king. King Willard has died and we have buried him. I am sorry you could not be here."

Rohn stepped forward and said, "You have killed my brother? I'll have—"

Axel interrupted him. "No. He had been sick for years. His passing was peaceful."

His dark face reddening with his furry, Rohn spat, "Your son and your wife won't have so easy a death." He threw his head back and laughed loudly.

Axel could feel the words strike against him like the blows of large stones. Rohn had not only Sid, but now he must have found out who Molly was and he had her, too.

The texture of the day and the composition of the forces he faced changed for Axel. It was as if the world had tilted and he were spilling off. There were no places to grab and hold on. All the things that had propped up his understanding of how things worked, were jumbled as they slid and shifted and crashed against him. He yelled, "If you harm either of them, I will see you dead, Rohn."

The black clad knight took one step toward Axel and, pulling his long battle sword, lifted it with both hands over his head.

Axel had no sword or shield. He knew he would live as long it takes for an eye to blink. Rohn would take the two steps that separated them and bring that long, heavy blade down, and it would slice most of the way through his body. He would plunder and burn this castle, then kill Molly and Sid.

Axel knew it didn't matter what he did, he was dead. He couldn't change that, but he could decide which way he was headed at the end. He charged at Rohn and saw the blade slicing down as he moved forward.

Just as Axel started to move, he heard that familiar twang and chunk, although this time the sound was deeper and very close, right in front of him.

Rohn's arms stiffened and the blade stopped its downward slice. Rohn's mouth stretched into a straight line, and his eyes got big when he looked down. There were feathers sticking out of his breastplate. The large man dropped his sword, slowly raised his hands and gently fingered the feathered shaft. He looked again at Axel as if he couldn't understand what was happening to him and pitched face down into the snow and dirt.

Grrr hadn't made it to Rohn before the bowman shot. When Rohn fell, Grrr returned to Axel's side.

Axel looked quickly at the bowman. He was watching the knights. He had no more shafts and was as unarmed as was his king.

Rohn lay on the snowy road, face down. There was no need to see if he Rohn was alive, a man center shot always died. Axel tried to think what this would mean for Molly and his son. Rohn was no longer lord of his castle. Would the people still there panic and leave? Were Molly and Sid locked away in a tower or dungeon? Bad thinking. They wouldn't know at Rohn's castle that he was dead. They would think that he was attacking Amory until someone rode to the castle to tell them.

But, the important thing was the decision Rohn's knights made right here. They could still attack the castle or they could return to their homes.

Axel saw that the two knights still on horseback and the one who had donated his armor were talking quietly together. They glanced at the castle then at Rohn's body and back at the army lined up in the road. Axel turned to face the castle, and all along the front parapet were men holding what looked like the new bows.

Axel couldn't hear the knights' voices, but he figured they were discussing whether to go back or to attack the castle. They could kill this young king now and take the castle in a few weeks. With their king dead, the knights in the castle wouldn't have anything to fight for.

Axel guessed that they had made up their minds for they walked back to the second row of knights and discussed it with them. They, too, examined the castle with its lowered drawbridge. Axel thought they were deciding whether they could get to it before it was raised.

The lead knight said something to one of the other knights and rode back along the column. In a moment the drum sounded again, only this time the pace was much faster, and the army began to shuffle forward.

Axel felt he wanted to but knew he couldn't run. The men on horseback would run him down before he was half way to the castle. If he stood where he was, he'd be trampled by the lead knights' war horses, huge beasts almost twice as big as plow horses. That left one thing he could do. Axel walked forward toward the row of knights. This was unexpected and they hesitated. Axel made a show of looking at the placement of the bowmen standing in the ditches at the sides of the road. Rohn's knights had to think that these men could kill them at will.

Some of Rohn's soldiers came forward and put Rohn's body on a stretcher and carried him toward the rear of the column. The lead knights again checked the distance to the castle and looked at each other.

It was time. They were going to rush the castle. They'd charge right over Axel and his bowmen. This had been a bad idea. The castle was open and would stay open as long as he was alive. He had left that instruction.

Axel stopped moving forward and turned his back on Rohn's men and looked at the thin track to the castle. On horses, Rohn's knights could charge up the spine of land leading to the big doorway and gain the castle before the gatekeeper had a chance to raise the drawbridge.

When Axel turned to face the knights, he saw them readying themselves. They were pulling their long battle swords and unstrapping their maces. Most of them had untied the shields hanging on their saddles. A few had even lowered the visors of their helmets. There was the sound of metal on metal all down the long column.

Axel walked quickly to the lead knight and said. "You may attack the castle, but at least twenty of you will die right here and within the next few minutes. You saw what the bow did to that armor." He pointed to the breastplate now lying at the side of the road. "Look at the men lined up on both sides of the road. There is more than one bowman for each of your knights. They will be the first to die. If the bowman have time to reload, then more of your soldiers will die here. Is that what you really want?"

The lead knight stared at Axel, then lifted his sword above his head, pointed upward, so that the men behind could see it. Axel knew that it was the signal to attack. If the men in the ditches had bows that would work, now would be the time for them to fire. Axel knew they couldn't and, along with him, would be some of the first men to die.

55

In a soft voice that he felt no one else could hear, Axel said to the bowman who had remained at his side, "When you get a chance, run for the woods. It's your only hope. They may want to get to the castle so badly they'll not chase you." The bowman's face was hard, and Axel knew he had already made up his mind about how he was to die.

Axel smiled at him as a way of acknowledging his bravery, but the man was looking past Axel and his face took on such an expression that Axel turned to see what he was seeing.

Coming from the direction of the beach and almost to the road was Rotug. He had painted his body blue and was carrying his huge axe. The knights, too, looked to see what Axel and the bowman were looking at with such intensity. When they saw Rotug, they realized that this was serious, for there never would be just one blue barbarian. The beach must be full of them. These knights had all fought the blue men or had heard of them and knew that this was a major problem for everyone.

From the coast where the cliff stopped and there was enough beach to pull up a small boat, at the place where the blue men had landed when they had attacked the kingdom the first time, came a high pitched cry immediately followed by another one almost identical to it.

The sea and most of the beach were hidden in snow that was blowing toward land and swirling wildly when it hit the beach. Out of these thick, white clouds emerged a large, dark head, then the neck, wings and body of a dragon. And another one just like it. Two dragons and they were supposed to be gone. There shouldn't be even one, and here were two of them.

Two dragons and an invasion of blue men at the same time. This was too much for any army to face. The forward movement of Rohn's army halted, first at the front where the dragons were seen by the knights, then the long column began to pile up as successive ranks bumped into the ones in front.

As soon as Rotug saw Axel standing alone and facing an army, he cried out and ran toward the line of men. Saddles creaked and metal rang on metal as the knights shifted their weight and readied their weapons preparing to fend off an attack. Axel said to himself, They must be Next and Next To Last. It's the twins when we really need them, or we're all in lots of trouble.

If Axel hadn't seen the twin dragons together and obviously with Rotug, he'd never have guessed that they were the twins that Sidney had raised and trained. They were almost twice as big as they'd been when he'd worked with them teaching them to drop eggs on the blue invaders.

When the dragons reached the road, about fifty yards from where it branched up to the castle and just in front of the lines of men, they settled down on the now white surface, shook the snow off their wings and folded them against their bodies. They sat in the road, side by side, and watched Axel and waited for instructions. Rotug caught up with the dragons and stood next to them and he, too, looked at Axel.

Axel turned to the head knight and said, "If you'll excuse me for a moment, I have to talk with my blue friend and his two friends." He walked the short distance to Rotug and, when he was close enough that the blue giant could hear him, said, "Rotug, I think you're just in time. Things were getting tense here. I was about to have to attack Rohn's army by myself." The dragons followed Axel's moves closely with their yellow, black-slitted eyes.

Axel didn't want to get any closer to the twins than he had to. Even though they had learned to trust him when they were young and small, they now were huge and might have forgotten who he was.

He stopped when he was close enough to Rotug to talk at a conversational level.

"Rotug and twins help."

"Things are looking much better now that we have you and the twins. How did you get them to come with you?"

"Twins. . .smart dragons."

"I know they are. You'll have to tell me all about it later. Now we have a problem with Rohn's army. Rohn's dead."

"Dead Rohn is good Rohn."

"But his army is just about to attack the castle. First they'll kill us, then they'll rush the gate. The castle can't hold out against them."

"Rotug help."

"Good. But what can we do? And what did you bring the twins for?"

"Sidney train twins to carry eggs and drop in sea."

Axel was impatient but tried to keep it out of his voice, "I know, Rotug, but we don't have that problem now."

Rotug nodded and continued, "Sidney and Axel train twins to drop eggs on Rotug's people."

"Sorry we had to do that, Rotug."

"Is all right. Rotug's people train twins to drop soldiers in sea like eggs."

218

Axel frowned, glanced back at Rohn's army and turned his head slightly to the side and said, "What do you mean?"

"You watch Rotug and hold axe," He held out the huge, double bladed weapon. Axel took it and it immediately hit the road. Axel couldn't hold it even using both hands. He leaned the handle against his body and looked at his friend.

The blue giant held one arm above his head and the twins intently watched this movement. When both dragons were concentrating on his arm, he pointed it at the line of knights and soldiers in the road to the side of where Axel stood. This action was familiar to Axel for Sidney had trained the dragons using those same commands. The dragons looked in the direction Rotug was pointing and then at Rotug. The blue giant pointed his arm at the water and cocked it back and forth at the elbow two times.

The twins looked at each other; it was almost as if they were discussing this new order. The dragons opened their huge wings and began to beat the air with them. The snow blew in clouds and the twins were lost in the whiteness for a moment as they slowly lifted. When they were above the churning clouds they had created, they flew toward the woods then made a circle over the lines of men.

The first dragon dove at the road closely followed by the second. A few archers fired arrows at the twins, but of course, those arrows that hit bounced off their tough scales. The men below the dragons dove for the sides of the road. The roadway was littered with the weapons they dropped. The dragons selected one soldier each from the hundreds lying in the snowy ditches, and, with cries, snatched them up with the talons on their front feet.

The twins flew toward the water and disappeared in the whiteness. The knights being carried cried and kicked and beat at the dragons, and when they couldn't be seen anymore, they could still be heard screaming. Axel was appalled. Were they going to drop the men in the sea and let them drown? "Stop them, Rotug."

"Rotug do that."

Axel turned and looked at his friend. Rotug had uncrossed his huge arms from over his chest and was reaching for his axe. "Rotug, I didn't mean stop Rohn's men, I meant stop the dragons."

"Dragons be back for more men in short time."

And they were. Out of the white mist of snow came the two dragons directly for the lines of men. The soldiers who had been in the ditch had climbed back to the road and now were collecting their weapons.

Their leaders were shouting at the confused and frightened soldiers as they tried to get them organized again. The dragons circled the road a second time. The lines of men again threw their weapons down and ran for the ditches.

Axel yelled at Rotug, "Rotug, stop the dragons."

The blue giant raised his arm in the air, and the dragons must have been keeping their eyes on him for they stopped circling and flew toward him. He dropped his arm and pointed to the road behind him, and the twins settled down again amid clouds of whirling snow.

56

Sidney had walked from the castle to where Rotug, Axel and the dragons were standing in the road. He asked Axel, "Will they go home now?"

"I don't think we want that, do we?"

"Sure we do, Axel," Sidney said, looking into his face. That's what all this has been about. Stopping Rohn and his army. . .What do you mean?"

"These men live in the kingdom, don't they?"

"Sure, they must live in or near Rohn's castle."

"I'm the king of all the people in the kingdom, aren't I."

Sidney was silent as he tried to understand what Axel was talking about. He wasn't sure, but he nodded his head.

"Then I'm their king, too. They have the right to have a king looking out for them just like the people in Willardville do."

"Yes, but. . ."

"There can't be special people in the kingdom. Everyone in it has to have the same rights to a king as everyone else. That's the only way I'll run things."

Sidney was surprised by what Axel said. He felt he knew him as well as any person can know another, but this was way past any thinking he'd expected. Axel was about to become a great king—if he wasn't one already.

Axel called Rotug over to him and told him to send the dragons out past the woods and out of sight. He didn't think the dragons would be needed any more, but he didn't want to take too big a chance. "You stay with them for the rest of today. If you hear the bell ringing, come to the castle at once. Bring the twins." He looked at all the blue on his friend and realized that the giant must be cold.

Axel said, "Take my cloak. I won't be needing it for a while," He handed his cloak to Rotug, who threw it over his shoulders. It was much too small but welcome just the same. The blue giant picked up his axe and headed for the woods. The dragons watched him, and when he was almost to the trees, he held up his arm, and the twins again beat the snow into twin tornadoes as they slowly rose to follow.

When Axel turned back to the knights, they had all dismounted and were in a group discussing their choices. Axel walked up to them and said in a voice loud enough to be heard over all of theirs, "We would like to welcome you to Amory. As you can see, we have set tables up with food and drink in anticipation of your coming. Mount your horses, give orders to your soldiers to camp there in the tents by the woods and come to the castle. After we eat, we can sit in the great room and tell each other lies."

There had been so much tension in the afternoon that this little bit of humor was a great release. The knights roared with laughter. The leader of the knights looked closely at the one standing next to him. This man nodded slightly.

The lead knight turned back to Axel and said, "Your Majesty, we accept your kind invitation, and would be honored to eat at your table and sit in front of a fire and tell you lies."

The knights laughed again and Axel joined them.

Before the night was out, all of Rohn's knights had pledged their fealty to King Axel. Although most of them decided that they'd continue to live in Rohn's castle, six of them wanted to come to Amory and live near their new king. Axel was glad to have them do this and welcomed them warmly.

As soon as the knights pledged allegiance to King Axel, he asked them about Molly and his son. The knights looked at him and didn't understand what he was talking about. When he explained that their new queen, Molly, had been selling dragon ears at Rohn's castle, they remembered her and told Axel that, yes, she had been there. They didn't know if she still was. The brightly painted wagon had been in the courtyard when they'd left with the army for Amory.

Axel knew he had to go to Rohn's castle as soon as he could. If Molly and Sid were there, he'd find them. If they weren't. . .he'd have to deal with that at the time.

Calling Sir Bruce and two of his new knights to his side, Axel asked them to accompany him to search for his wife and son. The three men were eager to help and called for their horses.

The knights were no longer in armor; they didn't expect to have to fight and soon the four men pushing their horses on their way north.

Within two hours they were in sight of Rohn's castle. It was a good bit smaller than Amory and wasn't as well situated for defense, but it was impressive.

The men who had been Rohn's knights had no trouble getting the guard to lower the drawbridge and let them enter.

Axel and Sir Bruce had ridden together and the two knights had followed them. Axel looked at the huge knight and asked, "Where would he put them, Sir Bruce?"

"I don't know, Your Majesty. Let's ask these men. They should have some idea."

223

Axel stopped the two knights just as soon as they were all past the large gate and entering the courtyard. "Where should we look?"

The two turned and looked up at the tower and talked quietly together for a moment. Turning to Axel, the older of the two said, "Sire, either in the tower or in the dungeon. I think that is the more likely place."

"The dungeon?"

"Yes, Your Majesty."

Axel couldn't imagine Molly and Sid in a dungeon. What an awful thing to do to such wonderful people. He still felt bad about Rohn's death, but now he had the guilty thought that maybe Rohn deserved it.

The four quickly found the stairs to the cells and, carrying a lantern, looked into each room as they came to it. No woman, no boy.

At the end of the corridor they found a cell door that was locked. Sir Bruce had taken a large key from a hook on the wall and he opened the thick door.

When the lantern lit the interior of the cave-like room Axel could see two people chained to the wall. He couldn't see well enough to tell who they were, but he was sure he had found his family.

The men who had entered the cell were behind the light and Sid couldn't see them clearly, but his wonderfully young but indigent voice yelled out, "You better let us go. My father will do bad things to you if you don't."

It was Sid. His brave son. Within moments Molly and Sid were freed from their chains and in Axel's arms.

57

In the morning, when Axel met Sidney in the kitchen, Rotug was with him. They were eating dragon ears and drinking milk. Sidney had put some crumbs on the floor for Cynthia.

Axel sat at the table with them and took a dragon ear from a large pan of them. "You like these, don't you, Sidney?"

Sidney had a mouthful, but that didn't stop him from saying, "I never had anything so good, even when I made it."

After washing some ear down with milk and wiping his upper lip clean of white, Axel said, "I'm going to have to make a decision. . .probably sooner than I want to."

Rotug had washed the blue from his body and looked like he usually did. He looked up from the plate of ears he was studying and said, "Rotug help more."

Axel laughed and said, "Thanks, Rotug, but this isn't that kind of decision."

Sidney put his elbows on the table with his hands under his chin and said, "What's the problem? Maybe I can help."

"I want Molly to be happy and I know she'll want to go back to the valley and so do I, but I can't live there and be king. And I have to be king."

Sidney remembered their conversation about this and he nodded. "You're right, Axel, you don't have a choice. And if you stay in Amory, that means Molly will have to stay here, too. If she's here, then Sid'll have to be here."

Rotug leaned forward and said, "Rotug stay with Sid and Molly and dragon ears."

They all laughed.

Sidney looked very serious and cleared his throat before he spoke, "I want to do something for you, Axel, for helping me save the kingdom this one last time."

Axel looked up with surprise. What could Sidney want from me? He'd never talk as if I'd helped save the kingdom if he weren't trying to get something for himself. He's kind and I'm sure he likes me, but he just wouldn't give something away.

Sidney continued, "You don't need money, but I can do something important for you. I can take care of the valley for you. I'll go back there and start my chicken ranch."

Axel shook his head and said, "I'll need you here, Sidney."

"What for?"

Axel thought for a moment and said, "For research."

Sidney frowned, and looking at Rotug, said, "I don't think there could much left to do research on. I think that most things that could be discovered, have been. I don't think I'll do that any more."

Molly walked into the kitchen and said, "Should the king be in the kitchen talking with just common folk?"

The men at the table laughed and she said, "When are we going home, Axel?"

Here it comes, thought Axel. "We are home, Molly."

"No we're not. We're at Amory. Home is where I have my own kitchen and my chickens and my cow and our house and our lake and our son. Home is the valley, Axel. Not this cold stone monster."

Sidney held his hands out on either side of the plate of dragon ears and said, "Axel doesn't have a choice, Molly. He's the king whether he or you like it or not. That means that the people of Willardville are counting on him. He can't take care of them if he's in the valley. He has to be here. And he has to be king. That's not a simple thing. Not just anybody could do it. All of us are now counting on him."

This was another long speech for Sidney to make and it doubly impressed him. But, it didn't impress Molly. She stood and said, "Axel, you decide what you want or have to do. Sid and I are going home. Come if you like." She walked from the room with her back very stiff and straight.

Sidney looked at Axel and said, "It's never over, is it old friend?" He shook his head and continued, "That's what makes it worth living. If it were easy, it wouldn't be fun. Molly'll see that she has responsibility here just as you do. Talk to her, Axel."

58

Later that evening as they were preparing to go to bed, Axel said, "Molly, you couldn't go back and leave me here, could you?"

Molly's back had been stiff and her hand gestures jerky and not at all soft and graceful ever since the conversation in the kitchen. Now she turned and faced her husband, and with a tight voice, said, "I don't want to live here, Axel."

"Why not?"

It would be like we were on display all the time. Everyone would be looking at us. We'd have to act the way they expect. We couldn't be us."

"That may be the way King Willard was, but it doesn't have to be that way with us. As king and queen we can be any way we want."

"What would we do?"

Axel threw out his arms wide and said, "Oh, there'd be lots to do."

"What?"

"We'd have to. . .you know. . . .Every once in a while there'd be. . .problems. . . . We'd have to solve them." Axel smiled.

"What problems?"

Axel had never thought of what he'd be doing as king. This might be a good a time to figure that out.

He sat on the edge of the bed and said, "Come and sit beside me, Molly." He patted the bed. Molly sat, but looked straight ahead and said nothing.

Thoughts raced through Axel's head and he had to straighten them out to help Molly understand. To give another person your ideas and have that person understand them the same way you do is really hard. Axel thought that the best way to do it was to start at the beginning and organize his thinking as he went along.

Axel started slowly with the thinking he had done up to that point on kings and leadership. "The main job any leader has is to protect the people who support him. The only other things leaders should do are those things that the people can't do themselves."

Axel was using his hands and fingers to keep track of his points. "Things like organizing the making of roads, arranging trade with neighbors, settling disputes, warning his people of troubles or dangers and encouraging them to learn to read. All the other choices of living should be left up to the people to decide for themselves." He held out his hands. "So, see, Molly, there would be all kinds of things for us to do."

"What about Sid? What would he do?"

"All the things he'd do at the valley, but here he'd have other boys to play with."

Molly looked at Axel, smiled and said, "And girls?"

Axel hadn't thought of Sid and girls. He now did and nodded his head. It was almost time for that, too. "Sure, Molly, in time, girls."

"Would we stay in this room or would we have a house or what?"

"We'd live in the king's chambers. We'd have the whole castle to live in if we wanted to."

This was sounding like it might not be too bad after all. "Could we have my father come and visit?"

Axel put his arm around Molly's shoulder and said, "Any time my mother can come with him."

They laughed together as they blew out the lantern.

229

59

The next morning Axel sent a guard to ask Rotug and Sidney to meet with him in the kitchen. When they were seated and eating dragon ears, Axel said, as he reached for another one, "There are enough of these things that we'll be eating them for months to come."

"Rotug like dragon ears for long time," Rotug mumbled around an ear.

Sidney took a drink of milk and said, "It's early, Axel. We were sleeping," and he reached up and ran his hand over Cynthia's black stubble, which caused her to open her eyes. "What's this all about?"

Axel sat forward and said, "I think Molly understands about me being king and that I have to live here instead of the valley. She's not happy about it, but she understands, and that's good."

Sidney dropped his head onto his arms on the table and his voice was muffled when he said, "You got me up to tell me that?"

"No. You two are my loyal friends, and I want to talk with you about what you're going to do." Axel turned to Rotug and asked, "What about the twins? You can't keep them here, you know. Can they find their way home?"

"Twins big dragons now."

Looking relieved, Axel turned to Sidney. "I think that you may be too old and your hands too twisted and sore to work a chicken ranch by yourself. I think it'd be a good idea if Rotug spent some time with you, at least until you got it set up."

Sidney was quiet for a bit. He was thinking about what it would be like living with the giant and his axe. "Would he have his axe?"

"Would it matter, Sidney?"

The wizard was silent for a moment, then, after he had looked up at Rotug, he smiled at Axel as he said. "No. I guess not."

Axel sat forward and asked, "Then, is it settled? You return to the valley, start a chicken ranch, Rotug goes with you to help, my family and I stay here and the twins go back home."

Sidney and Rotug were both picturing how it might be and, when they looked at each other, they nodded. Axel knew it would be fine now. Grrr, for some reason, barked.

Axel said, "Now you two can stay here as long as you want, and when it's time for you to go, you'll need horses and equipment. You can have anything here that'll help. Sidney, You'll need some stock to start with. Select what you need and I'll see that the farmers are paid."

Sidney thought for a moment and said, "I've been working on an idea for chickens with big thighs and legs and small wings. I think that if I find chickens with bigger legs and smaller wings and breed them, the chicks might have bigger legs and thighs. What do you think, Axel?"

This was a whole new idea for Axel and he didn't know what to think. In his mind he saw huge chickens, taller than a man, with little stubs for wings. There were about fifteen in a corral made of stout logs. They were jumping over the logs and Sidney was chasing them with a knife and frying pan.

"I think you should work on it, Sidney. You and Rotug."

Looking at Sidney's shoulder, Rotug said, "Rotug like chicken."

"You can take Winthton with you if you want to. I'll see that you have two strong horses to ride back and two good plow horses to use in the valley."

Sidney looked at his friend and said, "That's fine, Axel. Rotug could be help around the ranch." He was silent a moment, then went on, "You and Molly and Sid should plan on coming out to see me come summer."

"That's the agreement I made with Molly last night. We spend most of the year here in the castle, but we'll spend the summers at the valley."

"Where will you live when you come, Axel?"

Axel knew that this would come up and it was the tricky part. "In our house. You and Rotug will be living in the house you build first thing."

"Your house?"

"You haven't forgotten the bag of gold I handed you have you?"

Sidney turned and looked at the wall. He stayed that way for some time, and when he turned back he was smiling. "No. I haven't forgotten, my boy. I was just kidding." He laughed.

232

60

Axel and Sid stood on the part of the parapet that faced the sea. It was much warmer this morning, with a soft breeze from the south that had melted what snow had accumulated on the ground. The air blowing over the land held a warm dampness that made Axel think of spring and plowing.

He shifted his position so that he was leaning on the stone ledge with both elbows and had his legs crossed with most of his weight on the right one. Sid studied his father's position and posture and copied him. He had to stand on a step to do it, but when he had his elbows on the shelf, he crossed his legs in the same manner, and, after he had again checked his position, he, too, studied the water. The two stood like that for some time.

Sid put a package of dragon ears next to Axel's arm. "Mother says that everyone who lives in the castle has to eat at least two of these every day until they're gone." He pushed the package with his fingertips until it nudged Axel's elbow.

Axel pretended not to notice nor to hear his son. He was looking at the horizon line, a slight difference between the gray of the sky and water. Above that a string of thin clouds were taking on a shade of light pink that grew brighter as he watched. The sky just above this was turning from pale gray to light blue.

Looking at the water, Axel said, "Sid, a decision I made caused a man's death two days ago." When Sid didn't say anything he went on. "It was Rohn. I didn't kill him, a bowman did, but he died because a plan I created didn't work the way I wanted it to. So, I see it as my fault." Still no response from his son.

"I don't think there was anything I could have done to prevent it but I am responsible. I want you to know this and how it happened."

Sid looked at his father's profile and said, "Why?"

"It's important to me and so it's important that you understand. I've told you that I won't kill any more and here a man died because of something I did." Axel turned and looked at Sid. Now he was looking at his son's profile as Sid watched the sunrise.

"We've talked about how we make decisions, and I want you to understand how I came to make the one that cost a man's life."

"All right."

Now both were watching a spot of bright orange break the gray horizon line.

"I know you remember that we have values that we use to make all our decisions by. We check these every time we have to make important choices, and that's what I did this time.

"One of my values is that I won't kill and another one is the value I place on you and your mother. We talked about some values being more important than others, didn't we?"

Without turning his head, Sid nodded.

"I had to make a choice between values. Sometimes two values can't be held at the same time. It's very hard to do, but people have to make choices between them if they're in conflict." He turned and looked at his son. Sid nodded his head and his eyes flicked at Axel once, then he continued to look at the water.

"I decided that you and your mother are the most important things in the world to me, and that value was the one that had to be the first one I'd keep. I didn't want

234

anyone to die. I worked hard to keep it from happening, but it did. I just wanted you to know about it."

Sid turned and faced his father and said, "That man died because of me?. . . Does that make me guilty of killing him, too?"

Such a boy, thinking of his own responsibility and possible guilt. Axel's eyes filled with tears, and he turned away so Sid wouldn't see them when they ran down his face. When he could speak without his voice breaking, he said, "No, Sid. You had nothing to do with it. It happened because I loved you more than I loved that man's life. This may not make much sense now, but I feel better having told you."

Sid didn't say anything for a long time. Both of them watched the sun rise above the gray line of the horizon without talking or looking at each other. Both were thinking, at different levels, about responsibility, truth and how to tell important values from minor ones or even if there was a difference.

Sid looked at his father and said, "Where will I get my values from, Father?"

Such a hard question. Axel felt that he couldn't impose his values on his son. When the time was right, he could offer them to him, but that's as far as he could go and still know that Sid would be his own man some day.

He put his hand on his son's shoulder and said, "When it's time for you to choose, some of them you can adopt from me. Like the king adopted me. You decide that something that I believe would be good for you and you make that value yours. That has to be your choice. I can help you then by telling you what I value and explaining why I value it. Does that make sense to you, Sid?"

Sid was looking into his father's eyes and he nodded as he said, "I think I understand. You'll tell me your values and, when I'm old enough, I pick the ones I like. Is that the way it works?"

"That's it, Sid." Axel turned back to the water and continued. "The other values that you'll have in life will be ones you figure out for yourself. Unfortunately, there isn't any place where they're written out for us." Axel paused and thought about what he had just said, then continued. "It would be a lot easier for people if they were written, wouldn't it?"

Sid nodded his head. "Sure it would. How do I know how to pick the ones to use?"

This was hard for Axel. There were some rules he could explain to his son but they were complicated to understand. Axel watched the sun sparkle and shine on the tops of the waves as they rolled in from the horizon and crashed against the rocks below them.

"There are some things that are so true that they're obvious, Sid. We don't have to pick them, we just recognize that they're true."

"Could I use them to choose values?"

"Sure you could." This was better. He might have something here that his son could use. "There are three ideas that you can use. One is that people have to live together, and that means that any value you have should help other people have a good life together. . . . Understand?"

"Sure."

"Two is that we're smart and we can choose to do things based on our thinking and not just on our emotions or feelings of the moment. That one's harder to understand, and if it doesn't make any sense to you now, it will soon."

"I think I understand."

"Three is that it's important that we learn as much as we can so that we can continue to make good choices based on what we've learned.

Axel looked into his son's eyes trying to see understanding. "Have we got this all worked out, Son?"

Sid was silent for a time, then he said, "I don't know."

"What don't you understand?"

Sid shook his head. "I don't know."

"Have I left anything out?"

"I think there might be something."

"I skipped something?"

"More than one."

Turning to face his son, Axel said, "We've covered everything I can think of. I can't imagine anything we've left out. What haven't we finished?"

Smiling at his father, Sid opened the package and said, "Your dragon ears, Father."

AFTERWORD

In some of the books I've enjoyed reading, I've sometimes wondered what might happen to the characters when the stories were over. At times I've enjoyed stories so much I've even wished I could ask the authors what happens next. In this case, if you'd like to know, read on. If you don't care, this story is over for you.

It all works out as Axel plans it should. He, Molly and Sid stay at the castle. Sidney and Rotug return to the valley, and the dragons find their way home where the blue men live.

As you might have figured, Axel's good at the king business. We could see hints of it near the last of this third book when he has to make decisions as the castle is about to be attacked. Remember how he decides to act so the knights will stay calm? Think of how good he makes the bowman feel when he's so nervous he can't move. He's even thinking about this man's safety when he's sure that Rohn is about to kill him. He tells him to run to the woods.

Axel is a very popular king and dies when he's 83 years old. He's robust and healthy until he falls down the stairs when he's following Sidneyalso to the basement workroom to see what he's been inventing.

Sidney and Rotug return to the valley and start a chicken ranch. There isn't a market for chickens because everybody has a yard full of them and don't need to buy any.

Sidney does finally marry Marie, and they have a son, Sidneyalso. Axel and Molly take her with them one summer when they return to the valley. They go back to the castle in the fall, and Marie stays at the valley. As king, Axel can marry them and he's glad to do so.

Sidney tries breeding big legged chickens, but that doesn't work out at all. He can't ever find ones that have bigger legs than any of the others. He works at it for three years, and then when Rotug leaves to go back to Willardville, he spends his time studying and eating chicken, but he always keeps one for a pet. When he's truly old and dies, Marie buries him with his last pet chicken.

Axel names Rotug to be the ambassador at large (fitting I thought) to the blue men. That's how Rotug spends most of his life, dealing with the problems of trade with his old countrymen. There are some difficulties at first because they think he might have defected, but Sidney accompanies him to his old home one summer and convinces his people that he'd been captured and brain cleaned. This is the first time that phrase or one like it had ever been used.

Sid grows to be taller than his father and is good at reading and writing. He turns out so well that Axel is sure he'll be a wonderful king someday. He understands all that Axel has taught him about making decisions based on values, and he applies it to his life so well that he becomes a local expert in what Sidney called *ethics*. That's a word he makes up and some people use the same word even today, but many still don't understand how to apply Sidney's ideas to their lives.

The twins vanish, but on dark mornings there are reports of very large birds, or something, far out to sea calling to each other and swooping low over the waves.

FINAL NOTE BY AUTHOR

So, this story ends, and the ends of things are sometimes sad. For me, creating characters is like giving life to people, and, like now, when the story is finished, I feel as if my people have died or gone on to live in other places.

I have that feeling about Axel, his family and his friends. They are no longer constantly in my thoughts as they were when I was creating them. They've graduated from my creative process, and now, if they exist at all, it must be apart from me. It's as if I've given them away. Readers can re-create them in their minds, and they might live again as long as each reader is learning about them, but when each reader finishes the story, the characters must die again.

As I'm writing the final pages of this third book about these friends I've made, it's as if I'm attending the funeral of people I've known for years and known very well. Together we've decided what they'd do, changed our minds (wiped the slate/page clean) and decided they'd do things differently. We've faced problems together and solved some. We've argued about what we wanted. Some of these disagreements I've won, but some I haven't.

I've sat at my word processor and laughed at some of the things my friends have chosen to do. At times I've felt tears in my eyes as my friends faced some of the painful things that I, too, have faced.

But this has been mostly a happy time for me. If they live again in your memory, I'll be pleased that I've had a chance to share with you these friends of mine. If their thinking can be of any help to you when you face similar problems, good for you. They've helped me learn about myself, and I'd like to think that Axel and Sidney might be able to help you, too.